MW01127236

IS IT REAL?

THE LOCH NESS MONSTER

ALSO BY CANDACE FLEMING

*The Enigma Girls: How Ten Teenagers Broke Ciphers,
Kept Secrets, and Helped Win World War II*

*Crash from Outer Space: Flying Saucers, Alien Beings,
and the Mystery at Roswell*

The Curse of the Mummy: Uncovering Tutankhamun's Tomb

IS IT REAL?

THE LOCH NESS MONSTER

CANDACE FLEMING

SCHOLASTIC
FOCUS
NEW YORK

If you purchased this book without a cover, you should be aware that this book is stolen property. It was reported as "unsold and destroyed" to the publisher, and neither the author nor the publisher has received any payment for this "stripped book."

Copyright © 2025 by Candace Fleming

All rights reserved. Published by Scholastic Focus, an imprint of Scholastic Inc., *Publishers since 1920*. SCHOLASTIC, SCHOLASTIC FOCUS, and associated logos are trademarks and/or registered trademarks of Scholastic Inc.

The publisher does not have any control over and does not assume any responsibility for author or third-party websites or their content.

No part of this publication may be reproduced, stored in a retrieval system, or transmitted in any form or by any means, electronic, mechanical, photocopying, recording, or otherwise, or used to train any artificial intelligence technologies, without written permission of the publisher. For information regarding permission, write to Scholastic Inc., Attention: Permissions Department, 557 Broadway, New York, NY 10012.

Library of Congress Cataloging-in-Publication Data available

ISBN 978-1-339-03793-6

10 9 8 7 6 5 4 3 2 1   25 26 27 28 29

Printed in the U.S.A. 37

First edition, March 2025

Book design by Stephanie Yang

PART ONE

THE INVESTIGATION BEGINS

A large envelope appears in your mailbox. There's nothing written on it. No name. No address. There isn't even a postage stamp. But you know who it's from. You glance around to make sure nobody is watching, then hide the envelope under your jacket. You hurry inside and up to your bedroom.

Cosmos, your fox terrier, is napping on the bed. But he perks up when he hears you opening the envelope. He knows that sound. It's the sound of a new assignment.

You are an investigator for the Black Swan Scientific Investigation (BSSI) team. Your job is to unravel—if you can—the natural world's greatest mysteries.

Ghosts.

Sea serpents.

Aliens from outer space.

You've tackled them all by asking the right questions and looking for evidence. You are skilled at spotting lies and determining whether something you've read or heard is true. By using your powers of observation, questioning, and reasoning, you can unravel problems others find impossible to figure out.

So, what mysterious event will you be investigating this time?

Inside the envelope is a white paper folder stamped with big bold letters:

BSSI CASE FILE CONFIDENTIAL

All investigations start with a close reading of the Case File. Within its pages you'll find statements from witnesses, accounts from experts and the media, pertinent documents, and other important details and information.

You open the Case File, excitement zinging through your veins.

An unsigned note is paper-clipped to the first page. Just one sentence long, it reads:

IS IT REAL?

CASE FILE: WHAT LURKS IN THE LOCH?

An aerial view of Loch Ness in the Scottish Highlands shows the long, narrow loch with its steep shores and (right) a portion of the ring road that both the MacKays and Spicers were traveling on when they spied the monster.

THE FIRST SIGHTING, ALDIE AND JOHN MACKAY: APRIL 1933

On a bright spring afternoon in the Scottish Highlands, John MacKay and his wife, Aldie, turned onto a quiet country road that followed the shore of Loch Ness. Aldie MacKay rolled down the car's passenger window. A cool breeze ruffled her hair as she looked out at the loch's murky water.

Suddenly, she shouted, "Stop the car!"

John braked.

Aldie pointed.

Just offshore, *something* rose up . . . up . . . up from the water. Dark. Enormous.

Neither Aldie nor John had ever seen anything like it.

The creature rolled and dove for several minutes. Around it, the lake's dark water churned and boiled like a witch's cauldron. Minutes later, the beast plunged beneath the surface. Waves radiated from where it had just been and crashed across the loch.

The couple watched until the surface of the water stilled once more. Would the creature return? They waited for almost an hour. But nothing stirred.

At last, John put the car in gear. The couple drove home.

But the next day, they reported the sighting to Alex Campbell. He was the water bailiff, the law enforcement officer responsible for policing the loch. He was also a part-time reporter for the local newspaper, the *Inverness Courier*. He wrote up the MacKays' experience. Two weeks after the "monster sighting," his story appeared on the front page.

"Strange Spectacle on Loch Ness: What Was It?"

On Friday of last week, a well-known businessman who lives in Inverness and his wife (a University graduate), when motoring along the north shore of the loch . . . were startled to see a tremendous upheaval on the loch . . . The lady was the first to notice the disturbance, which occurred fully three-quarters of a mile from the shore . . . There, the creature disported itself, rolling and plunging for fully a minute, its body resembling that of a whale, and the water cascading and churning and simmering . . . Soon, however, it disappeared in a boiling mass of foam. Both onlookers . . . realized that here was no ordinary [animal], because . . . the beast, in taking the final plunge, sent out waves that were big enough to have been caused by a passing steamer [ship].

The article raised eyebrows. Most of the newspaper's readers had lived their entire lives on the loch's shores, and they'd *never* seen anything like that. Was it possible? Could there be an unknown monster living deep in the loch?

Locals doubted the account. Loch Ness was not lonely and remote. It was a busy, well-traveled body of water. Fishing boats and ferries crisscrossed its surface. And in the summer, hordes of tourists descended on Loch Ness to swim in its chilly waters, hike around its rocky shore, and cruise its dark, often choppy surface on crowded steamboats. If a monster *did* lurk in the loch, someone would surely have spotted it before this. It should have caused a long string of monster sightings. So where were they?

Some locals, looking for clues in history, turned to a book written around 700 CE titled, *The Life of Saint Columba.* Within its pages is a brief scene between a saint and a "water beast." As the tale goes, a holy man named Saint Columba arrived at a town near Loch Ness where the beast was terrifying the local people. The saint, in a display of supernatural powers, commanded the beast to be gone. Could it have retreated into Loch Ness? Some now claimed *this* was the first recorded sighting of the Loch Ness monster, but others disagreed. How could an ancient folktale full of magic, mystical creatures, and spine-tingling supernatural forces be evidence of anything? Besides, they asked, why hadn't anyone

seen the monster since then?

A representation of the "water beast" St. Columba was said to have vanquished from the River Ness around 1,300 years ago. This illustration is from the medieval book *The Life of Saint Columba*.

Some locals recalled two other monster sightings.

In 1852, terrified residents armed with axes and pitchforks had watched as two dark and monstrous shapes in the water moved closer and closer toward the shore. One resident had even aimed his rifle at the shapes. His finger was poised on the trigger when he realized he wasn't looking at a monster, but rather . . . a pair of ponies! Frolicking in the water, the animals had managed to swim an entire mile across the loch. The locals had laughed ruefully as the ponies splashed ashore. Obviously, their imaginations had gotten the better of them.

In 1868, another "monster" had washed up on the loch's shores. Beaked and blob-like, the carcass measured six feet. It created a stir among locals. Worried, people came from all over the area to look at the creature. Finally, a naturalist from Edinburgh arrived. After

Does this photograph of a Shetland pony swimming in a lake resemble a monster? Locals living at Loch Ness saw a similar sight and believed it was.

examining the body, he declared the creature to be . . . a bottlenose whale. It was obvious that someone had played a prank. Whales, the naturalist explained, could not live in the fresh water of Loch Ness. They needed salt water. The animal had to have been caught at sea, then dumped into the loch as a joke.

A beached whale like this one shown in a historical photograph was briefly mistaken by locals for a monster.

Could the recent article in the *Inverness Courier* also be a joke? Could the unnamed couple be lying?

The identity of the couple soon leaked. The MacKays were well-known and respected. They owned a hotel in Drumnadrochit, one of the villages on the loch. Surely, they wouldn't lie about something like this. Most locals decided that the couple's imagination had just gotten away from them.

The incident was all but forgotten, until . . .

02

THE SECOND SIGHTING, GEORGE SPICER: JULY 22, 1933

"George, what on earth is that?"

The fear in his wife's voice caused George Spicer to slam on the car brakes. Gravel from the road skittered beneath his wheels.

Ahead of them, something was crossing the road. Something big. And gray.

It was coming out of a tall fern on the right and heading toward Loch Ness, which lay directly to the left.

George took his foot off the brake. Cautiously, he drove closer.

The couple saw the neck first—long and snakelike. George thought the creature looked like a dragon or some prehistoric animal.

He braked again. His car now idled just two hundred feet away from the beast. Its neck arched high into the air, and it turned to look at them. The beast's head was small. To George's horror, it carried the limp body of a lamb in its mouth.

The monster kept moving. Now its huge body came into full

view. Covered in elephant-like skin, George estimated the beast to be thirty feet long. He couldn't see any feet, and it appeared the monster's tail was curved around the other side of its body, out of George's view.

George put the car into gear again and moved toward the beast. It, in turn, dove into the loch. Neither George nor his wife heard a splash. By the time they got to the spot where the beast had crossed, it was gone. Braking, George climbed from his vehicle and looked around. But there was no sign of the monster—no trampled ferns, no footprints.

A sketch based on what George Spicer claimed to have seen crossing the road in July 1933.

The Spicers drove home. From the safety of his London town-house, George wrote a letter to the *Inverness Courier* detailing his monster encounter. Appearing in the newspaper on August 4, the story created a stir. Another sighting! And this one close-up!

Spicer's claim that the monster was long-necked and dinosaur-like especially impressed readers. Could it be a long-lost living fossil, a surviving member of a prehistoric marine reptile family?

Scientist and writer Rupert Gould was intrigued by the story and decided to follow up. He interviewed Spicer just months after the encounter. Spicer repeated his story. That's when Gould noted that the monster sounded a lot like the "diplodocus-like dinosaur in [the film] *King Kong*." Gould had seen the movie months earlier.

A still photograph from the 1925 silent movie *The Lost World*, starring Bessie Love. A box office hit in Great Britain, it was one of the first films to present the idea of modern-day people encountering lost worlds filled with prehistoric creatures. Eight years later, when the MacKays and Spicers reported their sightings, the idea of a long-forgotten creature from the mists of time was not a novel one.

King Kong, a monster movie starring a giant gorilla-like creature, had opened in London that previous spring. It was an instant blockbuster. Lines to buy a ticket stretched for entire city blocks. Those who made it into the theater were often terrified by the movie's realistic depiction of man-eating monsters. They covered their eyes and cried out. At movie's end, they left "white and breathing heavily," wrote one newspaper reporter. No one had ever seen anything like *King Kong.* With its then-revolutionary special effects, it transported viewers to a lost prehistoric world filled with monsters. And it posed this question for the audience: What would happen if prehistoric animals met modern civilization?

Spicer admitted that he'd also seen the movie. And he agreed with Gould's observation. Yes, his monster "much

A movie poster advertising the 1933 blockbuster movie *King Kong,* a film that both terrified viewers and opened them up to the possibilities of living fossils.

resembled" the movie monster. Spicer's beast, however, had a longer and more flexible neck. Also, while Spicer supposed his beast had feet, he hadn't been able to see them.

Readers across Great Britain buzzed with excitement. Could it be? Was there a prehistoric creature in Loch Ness?

Was the monster a plesiosaur, a marine animal that lived approximately 200 to 66 million years ago? Many believed Nessie looked like the prehistoric reptiles pictured here.

03

THE THIRD SIGHTING, HUGH GRAY: NOVEMBER 12, 1933

After church, Hugh Gray took a walk along the loch. What a lovely day it was for November. The surface of Loch Ness was still as glass, and the sun's rays reflected off it. As Hugh approached the spot where the River Foyers enters the loch, he decided to take a picture. Luckily, he'd brought along his box camera.

Suddenly, something huge rose up . . . up . . . up out of the water.

"I did not see any head," Hugh later said, "but there was considerable movement from what seemed to be the tail."

Raising his camera, he snapped five black-and-white photographs before the object sank out of sight.

Oddly, and despite this extraordinary encounter, Hugh didn't rush to have his film developed. A whole week passed before he finally saw what he'd photographed.

The first four pictures were too blurry to show anything clearly.

The fifth, however, showed . . . *something*.

The photograph taken by Hugh Gray. Although blurry and indistinct, it is still considered by many to be the first picture ever taken of the Loch Ness monster.

Hugh claimed it was the Loch Ness monster.

So did the *Daily Record*, a national Scottish newspaper that published the photograph. Many readers puzzled over the image. They could make out very little in the poor-quality picture.

No matter. Other newspapers across the United Kingdom picked up the story and published the photograph as well.

Almost overnight, the country was gripped by monster fever. People everywhere clamored for news of the creature, and newspapers responded by sending dozens of reporters to the area. Film crews arrived, too, hoping to catch the creature on celluloid.

Meanwhile, hundreds of Boy Scouts and outdoorsmen descended on the area. Some ventured out onto the lake in search of the monster. Others set up observation posts on the shore, binoculars pressed to their eyes, eagerly waiting for the creature to show itself.

But the loch's dark waters refused to reveal its secrets, until . . .

04

MORE CLUES?: DECEMBER 1933

Snowflakes shifted into the dark waters of Loch Ness on the day world-famous big game hunter Marmaduke Wetherell arrived in Scotland. He came with maps and binoculars and a hunting bag made from the skin of a water buffalo (he claimed to have killed the buffalo himself). Inside the bag he carried a compass, calipers, a Swiss Army knife, and a measuring tape. What Wetherell didn't have, however, was his hunting rifle. He'd been hired by the *Daily Mail* to track down the Loch Ness monster, not kill it.

His arrival made big news. For years, British newspapers had covered his daring exploits in the Himalayan Mountains . . . the Amazonian rainforest . . . the African Serengeti. In those stories, Wetherell *always* caught his beast. The public believed he'd do it again.

Radio broadcasters and newspaper reporters covered Wetherell's every move. They reported on his meals and his hotel room, his immense confidence and his gray tweed hunting outfit. The only movements they didn't cover were the hunter's actual hunts.

Wetherell insisted he needed to scour the loch without reporters. He couldn't have the press tromping along behind him. Their questions and cameras would scare off the monster. He promised, however, that he would let them know the minute he found anything.

Big game hunter Marmaduke Wetherell (center) presses binoculars to his eyes as he scans the surface of the loch. To his left stands the water bailiff. On his right is his cameraman.

On his second day at Loch Ness, while walking along the shoreline, something caught his eye. He moved closer.

Animal tracks.

Big animal tracks.

Crouching beside them, he opened his bag and took out his calipers. He measured the footprints at nine inches across and two inches deep. His experienced eyes, he later claimed, had never seen anything like them. He believed they could only have been made by a very powerful soft-footed animal and estimated that the beast was at least twenty feet long.

The hunter followed the tracks. They led right to the water.

Here, at last, was the evidence the world had been waiting for.

Rushing back to town, he headed straight to a telephone and called the editor of the *Daily Mail*. The next day, the newspaper's front-page headline read:

MONSTER OF LOCH NESS
IS NOT LEGEND BUT A FACT

Meanwhile, Wetherell was giving a press interview that was broadcast via radio across Great Britain. "It is suggested that I have had phenomenal luck in finding definite trace in [just] days." This, he explained, was due to *skill*, not luck. Certainly, this proved he was the world's greatest hunter.

But the press wanted more. The editor of the *Daily News* insisted Wetherell make plaster casts of the footprints and send them to

London's Natural History Museum for analysis by the scientists there. Editors refused to pay the hunter until he did.

Just days before Christmas, a grumbling Wetherell made plaster casts of the footprints. Wrapping them carefully, he shipped them off to London.

The Natural History Museum was world famous for its taxonomic work—naming, defining, and classifying groups of biological organisms. The museum's scientists did so by searching for shared characteristics between organisms. And they had the museum's extensive libraries, as well as its 70 million specimens of plants and animals from around the globe, to aid them. If *anyone* could identify those footprints, it was the museum's scientists.

The scientists, however, didn't rush to examine Wetherell's work. It was the holiday season, and they were busy celebrating. Despite the public's great interest, the scientists said they would not have an answer until *after* the New Year.

Meanwhile, "Nessie," as the monster was now being called, was becoming big business. Advertisers raced to print monster-themed ad campaigns for everything from floor polish to breakfast cereal. Selfridges, a fancy London department store, ushered in their new line of cuddly, stuffed velveteen "Nessies" by holding a parade that featured a seventeen-foot-long plush Loch Ness monster. And

It didn't take long after the first sightings for businesses around Loch Ness to use the monster in their promotional materials. This postcard from circa 1935 pictures the places Nessie had supposedly been seen. The word "haunts" in this case means "hangouts."

British Pathé, a producer of newsreels, brought Nessie to the silver screen with a short film that appeared in movie theaters. Titled *I'm the Monster of Loch Ness*, it featured a silly song of the same title.

The film and song were a smash hit.

Even more monster hunters descended on Loch Ness. Restaurants and pubs were crammed, and there wasn't a hotel room to be found. Traffic jammed the shoreline road in both directions. The beast had become a boon to the locals, until . . .

05

THE MONSTER BUBBLE BURSTS: JANUARY 4, 1934

The Museum of Natural History's eagerly awaited results were in. Wetherell's tracks didn't belong to an unknown species of animal. They hadn't been made by a diplodocus or a plesiosaur. They'd been made by . . .

A hippopotamus!

A hippo track found in Africa. Could Wetherell have truly mistaken this for the footprint of an unknown animal?

The museum's director, Dr. Charles Tate Regan, broke the news. His staff of botanists, entomologists, zoologists, and paleontologists had carefully studied the specimen and were in complete agreement. The footprints were "definitely created by a hippopotamus," said Dr. Regan. Since hippopotamuses did not live in Scotland, the scientist believed the prints had to have been made by a "mounted specimen." In those days, sadly, it was common to make umbrella stands, jewelry, and other items from parts of once-living animals. Obviously, *someone* owned a hippo-foot specimen and had used it to carry out a hoax.

Reporters converged on Wetherell. Did he own a hippo foot? It made sense that a big game hunter would have such an object in his home. Was it him? Had he played a prank?

Wetherell insisted he hadn't. Someone else made those tracks, he said. They'd planted them for him to find. He demanded that the prankster come forward and confess.

But reporters bombarded him with more questions. Why hadn't Wetherell recognized the tracks when he saw them? As a big game hunter, he'd spent years in the parts of Africa where hippos live. He also claimed to be a highly skilled tracker. Surely, he'd know a hippo print when he saw one.

Wetherell refused to answer the question. Instead, he sneaked away from the Loch Ness area under cover of night and returned to his London home. He knew the newspapers were mocking him. His reputation was in tatters. The public was laughing at him. Wetherell shut himself away, too humiliated to appear in public.

06

THE MONSTER RETURNS: APRIL 21, 1934

That day, Londoners opened their morning newspaper to find a photograph splashed across most of the front page. It seemed to show the head and long neck of a large animal swimming in Loch Ness. Beneath it, a headline screamed, "London Surgeon's Photo of the Monster."

The photograph that appeared on the front page of London's *Daily Mail* in April 1934. Called the "Surgeon's Photograph" because Dr. Robert Wilson claimed to have taken it, this photo was accepted by many as proof positive of Nessie's existence. It also validated the notion that the monster was a plesiosaur.

The photo had allegedly been taken by Dr. Robert Kenneth Wilson, a highly respected London surgeon. And his story went like this:

He was driving along the road that ringed Loch Ness, his camera sitting on the front seat beside him, when he decided to pull over and stretch his legs. That's when he noticed a commotion on the loch's surface about two hundred yards from shore.

Dr. Wilson watched for a minute or so. Suddenly, something broke the surface.

"It was the head of a strange animal rising out of the water," claimed the doctor.

He dashed to his car and grabbed up the camera. After struggling down the steep slope to the water's edge, he focused his camera's lens on the beast.

Pop!

Pop!

Pop!

Pop!

He got off four photographs.

But had he captured anything? Wilson was eager to find out.

He immediately drove to Inverness and found a place that could develop his pictures—Ogstons pharmacy.

The pharmacy's clerk, George Morrison, developed the pictures.

Two were blank, and one was blurry. But the fourth photo was . . . sensational!

It showed a long neck, curving forward and ending in a small head. Its reflection on the rippling water was partly visible. And behind the neck . . . Was that a suggestion of the monster's back breaking the surface?

Morrison couldn't believe his eyes. As he handed it over to Wilson, he suggested the doctor take the picture to the newspaper. But not a small one, he said. Big news like this deserved to be published in a newspaper with lots of readers.

Dr. Wilson agreed. He sent it to the *Daily Mail* along with a letter detailing the story.

The editor of the *Daily Mail* published both Wilson's letter and a cropped version of his photograph.

The photo had an astonishing impact on the public. As countless other newspapers republished it on their front pages, it grabbed peoples' imagination. Many now believed a monster lived in Loch Ness.

Dr. Wilson's reputation cemented that belief. Back then the title of "surgeon" carried great weight. Here was a professional man, bound by the scientific rules of his vocation. This spoke to his honesty and uprightness. A man such as Wilson would never prank them like Marmaduke Wetherell had. If Dr. Wilson said the photo was genuine, that was good enough for press and public alike.

The public accepted the "Surgeon's Photograph" as proof that a monster lurked in Loch Ness. And based on the image—the arched neck, the small head—most believed it *was* a plesiosaur.

Dr. Wilson's photograph also validated those earlier sightings. If one accepted the photo as proof of the monster's existence, then one also had to believe that the MacKays, Hugh Gray, and the Spicers had seen the beast, too.

For many, the events of 1933–1934 established it: Nessie was real.

PART TWO

YOU INVESTIGATE

You come to the end of the Case File. Already, your brain is buzzing. You're eager to get started. What really happened back then? Uncovering the truth will be a challenge. But you're up for it. You are a seasoned investigator.

It's time to find answers.

You take out the necessary equipment: a case notebook (which can be as simple as a couple pieces of paper) and your BSSI Investigator's Handbook. This second item will come in handy. After all, even the best investigator needs a reference book from time to time. You can't be expected to remember *everything*. In fact, you decide to look up something right now.

07

FROM THE BLACK SWAN SCIENTIFIC INVESTIGATOR'S HANDBOOK

EVIDENCE

Evidence is the testimony, signs, and objects that make an investigator believe something is true. Evidence is gathered to prove a fact. It includes footprints, fingerprints, samples of hair and blood, statements from witnesses, photographs, etc. **Caution**: One piece of evidence is not enough to prove the truth.

There are two kinds of evidence:

DIRECT EVIDENCE	vs.	CIRCUMSTANTIAL EVIDENCE
A type of evidence that gives straightforward proof or disproof of a fact. This can include confessions, video or audio tapes, eyewitness testimony, footprints, fingerprints, hair and blood samples, photographs, etc. Direct evidence is seen as more reliable than circumstantial evidence.		A type of evidence that implies something happened but does not directly prove It. This type of evidence requires the investigator to put "two and two" together. The investigator must use questioning and reasoning to connect the evidence to the event or claim. This type of evidence is not as reliable as direct evidence but can be used to build a case against an event or claim.

A Sample Case:

Now that we know what evidence is, let's use that knowledge.

A farmer claims he saw a pink flying saucer land in his field. Evidence includes:

- A statement from a neighbor saying she saw strange lights in the sky around the same time the farmer claimed the spacecraft landed.
- Metallic debris scattered across the field.
- A half-eaten apple with unusual bite patterns that don't look as though they've been made by humans.

Is any of this direct evidence?

The neighbor says she saw lights, not a flying saucer, so her statement is circumstantial evidence. Yes, the lights *could* have been made by an alien spacecraft. The neighbor *did* see them around the same time as the supposed landing. But she never said she saw a spaceship, nor did she give a description of one.

The metallic debris *could* have been left by a spaceship. It also could have been left by a passing satellite, an airplane, or even a prankster. Further tests by scientists are required to determine if there is anything otherworldly about the debris. For now, the evidence is circumstantial.

And the half-eaten apple? It *might* have been chewed by aliens. But when investigators ask questions, they discover the apple was chewed on by the farmer's son, who wears braces on his teeth. He tossed the apple into the field after discovering a worm inside it. The apple is no longer evidence. It has nothing to do with spaceships.

Remember: One can have evidence without having proof. That's because **proof** is when something is shown completely to be true through data, information, and fact. **Proof** establishes certainty and truth beyond a reasonable doubt. Example: We have *proof* that dinosaurs walked the earth 65 million years ago. We have *evidence* that a spaceship landed in a farmer's field.

Where should you start your investigation of the Loch Ness monster? You decide to start by looking at the **physical evidence.** Physical evidence are clues that can be seen or held. Does this case have any? You list them in your notebook:

1. The photograph taken by Hugh Gray

2. The photograph taken by Dr. Robert Kenneth Wilson

3. The plaster cast of footprints made by big game hunter Marmaduke Wetherell

Should you bother with the last item? Scientists at London's Natural History Museum debunked the footprints back in the 1930s. Did they have the knowledge to properly analyze the prints?

You read back over the Case File. It's obvious that the scientists working at the museum were highly knowledgeable. You feel confident accepting the scientists' conclusions. The prints *were* made by a hippopotamus.

A hippopotamus in Scotland?

It seems far-fetched, but as an investigator, you follow *every* lead. You don't decide if something is true or not until you have all the facts. You never make assumptions.

You flip open your computer and log in to the BSSI database. You search: "hippopotamus + environment." Your answer appears on the screen:

The hippopotamus (*Hippopotamus amphibious*) **is a large, semi-aquatic mammal found in sub-Saharan African countries. Hippopotamuses spend much of their time in water—lakes, rivers, and mangrove swamps—which helps them stay cool in the hot, tropical climate where they live.**

Scotland is not a place hippos can survive. You're not surprised, but you're glad you double-checked.

Now you look back at Wetherell's statement about the hippo tracks. He claimed that someone had placed them there for him to find. You ask, who might have played such a prank? And just as importantly, is there anyone who had something to gain from the hoax?

You immediately consider Wetherell. He loved attention and being famous. Finding evidence of the Loch Ness monster would have made him a celebrity around the world.

This information leads to another question: As a big game hunter who pursued animals in Africa, did Wetherell have access to a hippo foot? How can you find out?

It's a long shot, but you turn back to your computer. This time you search the database for "hippopotamus foot + Wetherell."

Bingo!

The hippo foot ashtray once owned by Marmaduke Wetherell, now on display at the Loch Ness Centre in Drumnadrochit, Scotland.

It's a picture of a hippo foot ashtray once owned by Marmaduke Wetherell!

Can you now conclude that the hunter played a hoax?

No, you need to investigate a little further to know for sure. Yes, you've uncovered evidence. But it isn't proof. Is it possible someone else had a hippo foot? It seems they weren't all that uncommon in the 1930s. Is it possible a Loch Ness local made the tracks? Why? Did they have something to gain? Sometimes people play pranks for the simple thrill of "pulling one over" on someone. But sometimes there are other reasons. Did someone want to make Wetherell look like a fool? Or did they want to grow the monster story so more tourists would come to the lake? You know from your Case File that the tourist industry had boomed because of Nessie sightings.

Hmmm.

The best way to prove Wetherell's guilt would be to talk with him. If he confessed, that would be proof. Sadly, the hunter died long ago.

You sigh. Sometimes investigations hit a dead end. You may never know who faked those prints.

But just because someone staged such a hoax doesn't mean that Nessie isn't out there.

It's time to break for a snack. Kibble for Cosmos. Blueberries for you. Brain food for both dog and investigator.

Q

Now, let's turn to the photographs. You look at Hugh Gray's picture first.

You can't help but make a face. True, photography in the 1930s wasn't as advanced as it is today. But this picture is poor . . . *really* poor.

Still, you think you can just make out the outline of a monster.

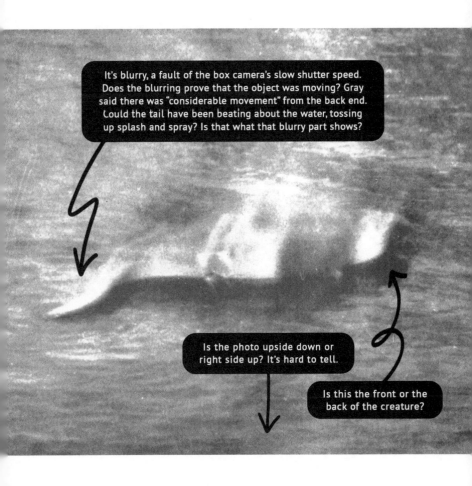

Gray said the head of the monster was under the water, but there was lots of activity coming from its back end, or tail. You peer through your magnifying glass. Yes . . . yes . . . look at that!

You think you see Nessie.

You *want* to see Nessie.

It would be so amazing if a prehistoric animal truly was living in Scotland . . .

Wait!

You take a breath, put down the magnifying glass, and recall a page from your BSSI Investigator's Handbook.

08

FROM THE BLACK SWAN SCIENTIFIC INVESTIGATOR'S HANDBOOK

BEWARE WISHFUL THINKING

As a BSSI investigator, you are searching for the answers to some of our most perplexing mysteries. Many of you may be eager to uncover the truth. Who doesn't want to prove that ghosts or extraterrestrials or mermaids really exist? But you must be careful. You have to be extra doubtful because you need to be on guard against your own wishful thinking.

How many times have you really wanted to believe something? Perhaps you've wanted to believe that the light on your ceiling was an angel, or that a mummy's curse was real, or that your next-door neighbor was a werewolf. And when you really, really, *really* want to believe something, you might latch on to whatever flimsy evidence you can find to bolster the claim.

And it could be. But you know you need *proof,* not wishful thinking.

Bottom line: The more you want to believe something, the more you should question and doubt it.

You close your handbook and think for a few minutes. Then you pick up the magnifying glass and look at Gray's photograph again. You're not searching for Nessie this time. You're just looking with a mind that is open.

You see . . . an otter!

And now . . . a swan!

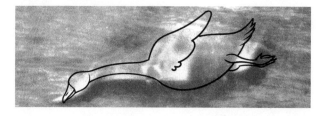

And now . . . a dog swimming with a stick in its mouth!

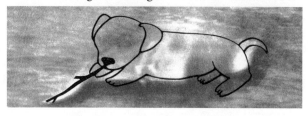

There is a scientific reason for seeing all this. It is a phenomenon called pareidolia (par-i-doh-lee-a). Pareidolia is a trick of the human brain in which a person sees something significant in a random image. It's the reason people have seen:

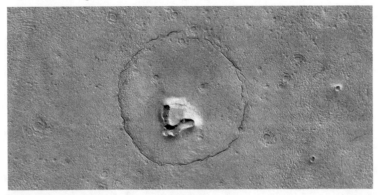

A teddy bear on the surface of Mars.

A face in the dish sink.

As much as you dislike admitting it, you realize you can't prove anything from Gray's photograph. You put it aside. It is another dead end.

You need another break—some exercise. You call to Cosmos. You both could use a walk around the block.

🔍

You're fresh and ready to investigate the "Surgeon's Photograph." Magnifying glass in hand, you take a close look.

It is a bit blurry around the edges, but the object is clear.

Is that a glimpse of the monster's back?

Clearly, the creature is moving against the current. But why do the ripples look so big in comparison to the creature?

Does this perfectly straight section of the neck look fake? Are you imagining that because of your previous experience with the Gray photograph?

You flip back to your Case File and reread George Spicer's statement. The only witness to see the monster out of water, he claimed it looked like a plesiosaur.

You pull up this picture online:

A vintage illustration of a plesiosaur. The plesiosaur once flourished in the earth's oceans 66 to 200 million years ago. A marine mammal, it had a small head; a broad, flat body; and a very long, flexible neck. Despite the awkward appearance of its body design, scientists believe the plesiosaur was a swift and graceful swimmer because of its four paddle-like arms. Unlike most other reptiles who lay eggs, the plesiosaur gave birth in open water. A carnivore, it ate fish, clams, squid, and snails.

Does the object in Wilson's picture resemble a plesiosaur?

Is Wilson's photo proof that Nessie exists?

You sit back. The photo might be real, but you need more evidence. It would be great if you could talk to Dr. Wilson about the photo. But he, too, is long dead. Hmmm . . .

Who did Dr. Wilson talk to about his photograph? You know what he told reporters at the *Daily Mail*. But who else did Wilson talk with? He must have been interviewed by lots of journalists. After all, both he and his photo became world famous.

You log back in to the BSSI database. You search: "Robert Kenneth Wilson + Loch Ness + interview."

Strange! Nothing comes up. As far as you can tell, after that first interview, Dr. Wilson never spoke publicly about the Loch Ness monster again. He didn't give any more interviews. He didn't provide any more details.

You try again. This time you search: "Surgeon's Photograph + Loch Ness monster."

You get lots of hits. You scroll through screen after screen. Every entry includes Dr. Wilson's photograph—the same one you've been investigating. But on the bottom of the third screen, an image catches your eye. It's the "Surgeon's Photograph," but it looks different.

Is that a shoreline along the top of the image? You look closer.

It is!

That's not the picture that was published in the *Daily Mail*.

To be sure, you compare them side by side.

They are identical except for the shoreline. Does it matter? Does the inclusion of the shoreline change anything?

As you stare at the images, it dawns on you. Inclusion of the shoreline gives everything a new sense of scale. Compared to it, the object in the water looks small, not more than a few feet long at the most. Hardly monster-sized!

Where did this second photograph come from? You read back over the Case Notes once . . . twice . . . looking for a clue to this mystery.

Eureka! You find it.

The *Daily Mail* published a *cropped* version of the photo. That means the outside edges of the image were removed to improve its framing and make the object look more dramatic. But by cropping the picture, it also skewed its scale, making the object appear much, much bigger than it really was.

There aren't two separate photos. There are two versions of the same photo.

Do you still think there's a real-live monster in the photograph? Is it possible Dr. Wilson was lying about his Nessie encounter? Is it all a hoax?

You turn back to your computer. This time you search: "Robert Kenneth Wilson + hoax."

An old newspaper article appears on your screen. It's from the front page of the London *Sunday Telegraph* and is dated March 13, 1994. Here's what you discover:

Ninety-three-year-old Christian Spurling had a confession to make. For most of his life, he'd kept a dark secret about the "Surgeon's Photograph." But now, fearing he'd take the truth to his grave, he wanted to come clean. "It's not genuine," Spurling told reporters. "It's a load of codswallop and always has been."

Spurling, the stepson of big game hunter Marmaduke Wetherell, claimed his stepfather had seethed with resentment after the *Daily Mail* made him a laughingstock over those hippo tracks. And he'd vowed revenge. "All right," Wetherell said to Spurling. "We'll give them their monster."

It was Spurling, along with his stepbrother, Ian Wetherell, who'd built the model monster. After creating the head and neck of the monster, they attached it to a windup toy submarine. When they finished, their creation looked like this:

A sketch of the monster model described by Christian Spurling.

Then Ian Wetherell and his father drove to Loch Ness and found an inlet with tiny ripples that could be made to look like full-sized waves if properly photographed. Ian took five shots before Marmaduke Wetherell intentionally stepped on the model. It sank into the lake. Afterward, the undeveloped film was given to a friend of the hunter's, Maurice Chambers, who handed it off to Dr. Wilson. It was Wilson's job to be the credible front man for the hoax. He agreed to do it, said Spurling, because the doctor loved a good practical joke. No one expected all the publicity that sprang up around the photograph. It scared all those involved so much that they vowed to keep the whole episode very quiet . . . until now.

Does this testimony *conclusively* prove that the "Surgeon's Photograph" is a fake? Is Spurling's story direct evidence or circumstantial evidence?

How does Spurling's story fit with other pieces of evidence you've uncovered?

Do you wish you had just a bit more physical evidence? According to Christian Spurling, the model is gone, sunk in the loch by Marmaduke Wetherell. But are there blueprints or sketches of the model? Is there a receipt showing the purchase of a toy submarine?

You shake your head. It appears there is no more physical evidence.

What about Christian Spurling?

Is there any way to confirm how truthful his story is?

Is there any way to know if he's left out important details or exaggerated parts of his testimony?

How did he know what happened at the loch? In his statement, he said he hadn't gone along. Did someone else tell him that part of the story?

Can you simply trust that his memory is correct?

Hmmm . . . you *did* find lots of compelling circumstantial evidence. What does that evidence lead you to believe? Why? Would you say the "Surgeon's Photograph" is a fake, or real?

Cosmos barks. It's time for lunch.

🔍

Now you're ready to turn to the witnesses. A witness is someone who saw something that happened or can give a firsthand account of an event. Who are the witnesses in this case?

John and Aldie MacKay.

Hugh Gray.

George Spicer and his wife.

Dr. Robert Kenneth Wilson.

You decide to take both Dr. Wilson and Hugh Gray off your list. You've already analyzed their photographs, and therefore their claims. That leaves just the MacKays and the Spicers.

09

FROM THE BLACK SWAN SCIENTIFIC INVESTIGATOR'S HANDBOOK

WITNESSES

He Said/She Said/They Said

Just because a person says they saw something doesn't mean it's true. When examining eyewitness testimony, it's important to listen for:

Fact: Something you can verify. *Examples*: 1 + 1 = 2; Earth is a planet that revolves around the sun.

Opinion: A personal belief. *Examples:* Beagles are the cutest breed of dog; Reading is more fun than playing baseball.

Assumption: Something that is accepted as truth without proof. While assumptions *might* be true, they should always be questioned and double-checked. *Examples:* Kids hate broccoli; Teenagers are lazy.

Lies: An untruth that is told on purpose. *Examples:* A salesman claims the chairs in his store are stuffed with Bigfoot's fur; A school-mate insists she has a pet dinosaur at home.

It's important not to confuse the above. Confusing them may lead you to the wrong conclusions.

It's also important to remember that human memory is faulty. Scientific studies have shown that humans perceive things selectively. They miss important details, mix up other people's descriptions with their own, and sometimes even add events that didn't happen. They don't do this on purpose. They are not lying. They are speaking what they believe is the truth without realizing their memories are inaccurate.

You start with John and Aldie MacKay. Are they credible witnesses?

You look back at your Case Notes. The *Inverness Courier* described John MacKay as a well-known businessman and Aldie as a university graduate. The newspaper reporter seems to be implying that they are reputable people. But is knowing their background enough for you to believe their story?

You also notice that the MacKays didn't rush to tell newspapers about their sighting. Instead, they reported it to the water bailiff, Alex Campbell, who published their story in the *Inverness Courier*. You wonder: Did the MacKays ever talk to anyone else about their monster encounter?

It's a good thing you have such an excellent database . . . and that you know how to search it. You put in: "Aldie MacKay + Loch Ness + interviews."

An article pops up.

You open it. It was written by Rupert Gould. Haven't you heard that name before? You review your Case Notes. Yes, there it is . . . Rupert Gould was the scientist and writer who talked with one of the other witnesses, George Spicer. Gould questioned Aldie MacKay not long after he spoke with Spicer. Here's the first part of that interview:

R.G.: Tell me what happened.

A.M.: My husband was driving. At one point in the road I caught sight of a "violent commotion" about one hundred yards [about the length of a football field] away from shore. I thought at first it was "two ducks fighting." But on second thought, it seemed like too much commotion for ducks.

You pause. Fighting ducks? You open a new tab and search for photographs of ducks fighting on a loch. You find:

Could the MacKays have mistaken *this* for a monster? They weren't looking through binoculars, and a football field *is* a long distance. This leads you to a new thought. Have other objects been mistaken for the Loch Ness monster?

The answer, after you do a quick search, is "yes." Among the items: Cormorant.

Seals.

Logs.

You remember something from your Case Notes. You add:

Swimming pony.

Dead whale.

Now you return to Gould's interview with Aldie Mackay. You read the rest of it:

R.G.: If not ducks, what did you see, Mrs. MacKay?

A.M.: The commotion ended, and I could see a big wake as if a ship had just passed and left behind waves. "Apparently it was caused by something large moving along just below the surface." Then, about the middle of the loch, about 450 yards away [a little more than three football fields], "the cause of the wake emerged, showing as two black humps moving in line, the rear one somewhat the larger."

R.G.: Then what happened?

A.M.: "The two humps moved with the forward rolling motion of a whale or porpoise." They showed "no traces of fins . . . they rose and sank in an undulating motion, but never went entirely out of sight."

R.G.: Can you estimate the creature's size?

A.M.: About twenty feet.

R.G.: And then?

A.M.: It continued to move for some distance before "swimming in a half-circle and sinking suddenly with considerable commotion."

R.G.: Why didn't you immediately report your sighting to newspapers? And why did you insist your names not be mentioned in the *Inverness Courier* article?

A.M.: I didn't want people to think I was "self-advertising" our hotel.

R.G.: Thank you for talking with me.

A.M.: You're most welcome.

You read the interview again. Then you flip back to your Case Notes and read what the MacKays first reported. The stories aren't the same. You need to compare them.

You make a simple chart in your notebook like this:

FIRST REPORT	SECOND REPORT
churning water	violent commotion
whale-like beast	beast swam like a whale, but wasn't a whale because it didn't have fins
beast dove and disappeared beneath the surface	beast never went out of Aldie's sight
no other physical details	two black humps, the rear hump was bigger
no estimate of size	twenty feet long
rolled and played in the water	swam for some distance before swimming in a half-circle and submerging

Why is the second account so different from her original one? Is Aldie MacKay lying? If so, which time? Or could this be an example of faulty human memory? The MacKays must have read or heard about George Spicer's extraordinary encounter. Could she have mixed up his details with her own memories?

Aldie MacKay certainly sounds credible in the Gould interview. She gave calm, thoughtful answers and explanations for her actions. She wasn't evasive or overly dramatic. She sounded truthful. Still, you know that when witnesses give inconsistent stories, their reliability must be questioned. You will probably never know why

Aldie MacKay's story changed. Still, as an investigator, you have to decide. Should you believe her? Why, or why not?

Cosmos is whining. You open the back door. You wait while he sniffs and pees. But something is nagging at you. You're missing something.

"Hurry up, boy!" you holler.

He trots inside just as you shout, "Eureka!"

🔍

Here's the question that'd escaped you: Why weren't there any monster sightings *before* the 1930s? Sure, there is an ancient book titled *The Life of Saint Columba*, but that's a story, not a sighting. You shake your head. It doesn't make sense. People have lived near the loch for centuries. Fishing boats, ferries, and tourist charters have long crisscrossed its waters. Shouldn't there have been thousands of sightings *before* the MacKays'?

You need to learn about the loch—its geography and history. To do that, you'll need an expert.

10

FROM THE BLACK SWAN SCIENTIFIC INVESTIGATOR'S HANDBOOK

THE KNOW-IT-ALLS: EXPERTS

Experts can come in handy during your investigation. An expert is a person who has skill, experience, or knowledge about a particular subject. They can explain information, supply little-known facts, fill you in on the newest data and studies, and provide unique perspectives. **For example:** You are investigating the possibility of life on other planets. You've come to the point in your case where you need expert help. You consider contacting an astronomer, an astrophysicist, or a deep space exploration scientist.

But scientists aren't the only experts. Beekeepers are experts on honeybees. Police officers are experts on law enforcement. Soccer players are experts on soccer. Who might have special knowledge of your subject?

Keep in mind that not everyone who *appears* to be an expert is one. It is easy to get fooled, especially if the topic is science or the law or other subjects most of us don't know much about. It's easy to manipulate technical-sounding language and data. Fake experts are good at making nonsense sound logical.

Your intelligence has nothing to do with whether these tricks can fool you. Good investigators always make sure experts are reliable before contacting them.

Red-Flagging So-Called Experts

1. You are investigating a mysterious virus. You read an article written by an oceanographer claiming that all medical doctors are wrong about the virus. **Red flag:** While the oceanographer *is* a scientist, she is *not* a disease expert. You should find another expert.

2. You are interviewing the author of a book about UFOs. He gives you few specific details. Instead, he says, "Everyone knows," and "My people have found," and "Other experts in my field say my theories are sound." **Red flag:** Who are the author's experts, his people, everyone? These statements are fluff, not proof. You should find another expert.

3. You are searching for evidence of paranormal activity in the Bermuda Triangle. You telephone the owner of the Bermuda Triangle Museum. She invites you to visit her museum. "Admission price is ten dollars," she says, "and I have a wonderful gift shop. I guarantee you'll leave believing that all the mysterious stories are true." **Red flag:** The museum director is making money from selling the idea that the Bermuda Triangle is real. That's a conflict of interest. You should find another expert.

4. You've contacted an author who believes giants built the Great Pyramid. He's written a book about the subject and given television interviews. He's gotten lots of attention because his ideas argue against what mainstream Egyptologists believe about the pyramids. You do an online search looking into the man's credentials. You notice that he doesn't list his education. You look closer and discover that he never received a degree in Egyptology. He just calls himself an Egyptologist because, as he says, "I've done my own research on the subject." **Red Flag:** That's not what research is. When Egyptologists and other scientists use the word "research," they mean a systematic process of investigation. Evidence is collected and evaluated in an unbiased, objective way, and those methods are made available to other scientists for scrutiny and replication. On the other hand, when someone says they're doing their own research, it typically means they used a search engine to find information that confirms what they already think is true. Yes, information is available, but that doesn't mean the so-called Egyptologist has the background knowledge to understand it.

Remember to be polite when contacting experts. They are doing you a favor by sharing their expertise.

You'll also want to think carefully about your questions before reaching out to an expert. Ask for information you can't find anywhere else. **For example:** You are investigating the disappearance of world-famous pilot

Amelia Earhart. You contact an author who has written a nonfiction book about the pilot's life. Rather than asking your expert for the date Amelia went missing (a fact easily found in books or online), you might instead ask what she thinks happened to the pilot and what evidence she has to back up her opinion.

Last, but not least, thank your expert for their time and expertise. Who knows? You might need their assistance with a future investigation.

You're ready to contact an expert. But who? Is there such a thing as a lake expert? You look it up online. There is! A scientist who studies lakes is called a limnologist. Limnologists examine a lake's biology, chemistry, and physics to uncover its secrets.

Have limnologists studied Loch Ness? Your computer keys click as you search for the answer in your database. Yes, lots of limnologists have examined Loch Ness. One catches your eye. Not only does she teach limnology at a Scottish university, but she spends every summer on the loch gathering data. She's even written several books about Loch Ness. Is she a reliable expert? You decide to email her.

To: Limnologistln@scottcollege.edu

Date: February 28

Subject: Questions about Loch Ness

From: You

Dear Professor:

I am an investigator with the Black Swan Scientific Investigation team. Right now, I am working on a case about the Loch Ness monster. Do you have time to answer a few of my questions about the lake? I can email them or call you if that is easier.

Thank you for your time.

Sincerely,

You

You look over the email before sending it. Is everything spelled correctly? Have you been polite? Satisfied, you hit SEND.

You cross your fingers. You really hope the scientist has time for your questions.

But what are those questions? What do you really need to know? You're brainstorming possibilities when your computer dings. It's a new email . . . from the limnologist.

To: You

From: Limnologistln@scottcollege.edu

Date: February 28

Subject: Questions about Loch Ness

Dear You:

I'd be happy to answer your questions. I happen to have a few free minutes now.

Please feel free to call me at +44 77-888-5454.

All the best,

Dr. Limnologist

"Stay quiet, boy," you tell Cosmos. Then you dial the scientist's phone number. Below is a transcript of that call:

You (Y): Thank you for taking the time to talk with me.

Dr. Limnologist (L): I'm really pleased to help. What do you need to know?

Y: I'm curious about Loch Ness's geological characteristics. Is there anything unique or special about it? Is it different from other lakes?

L: *[Laughs.]* Loch Ness is a mystery in itself.

Y: What do you mean?

L: For starters, it's twenty-three miles long and 788 feet deep at its maximum depth. That makes it the second largest lake in Scotland in terms of distance from shore to shore. But it is deeper and holds more fresh water than all the lakes in the United Kingdom combined.

Y: Wow!

L: The loch is connected to the North Sea by the River Ness as well as by a man-made waterway called the Caledonian Canal. Wait, let me text you a map so you can see what I'm talking about. *[The sounds of clicking keypad taps can be heard.]*

Y: *[Your phone dings, letting you know you've received a text. You take a minute to open it.]*

L: Got it?

Y: Yes, thank you.

L: You can see how long and narrow Loch Ness is—long, narrow, and deep.

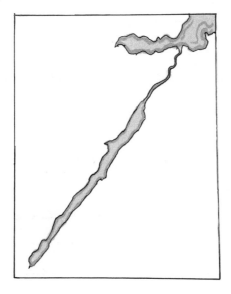

Y: Yes, I can see that.

L: What you can't see is how dark the water is. Peat from the surrounding hills is carried into the lake by the frequent Scottish rains, turning the water black. Visibility is poor at the lake's surface. But dive down thirty feet, and you won't be able to see a thing.

Y: Darkness like that could make it easy for a big creature to hide, right?

L: It could, but . . .

Y: You've spent years studying the lake. Do you believe a prehistoric creature could have survived there?

L: You mean like a plesiosaur?

Y: Yes.

L: May I tell you three more facts about Loch Ness?

Y: Please.

L: Fact number one: Scientific studies have shown that there are only about twenty-two tons of fish in the lake. This might sound like a lot, but it would be nowhere near enough to sustain a plesiosaur.

Y: Could the monster eat both plants and animals? You know, an omnivore.

L: Here's fact number two: Loch Ness is cold—forty-one degrees Fahrenheit all year round. It never warms up and it never freezes over. Reptiles can't live in an environment that chilly. Because they can't regulate their body temperature internally, they rely on the temperature of the environment around them. This gives them the energy to move around and hunt for prey.

Y: So cool!

L: You want to hear something even cooler? Most reptiles breed by laying eggs on the ground. But that isn't a good idea in Scotland, where the climate is colder. So, the adder, the only snake in Scotland, has adapted. Instead, the adder keeps its eggs inside its body, where it's warmer, and gives birth to live young.

Y: *[You are quiet a moment, thinking.]* Is it possible the Loch Ness monster could have adapted over millions of years in the lake?

L: *[Laughs again.]* I like how you think. That's a good question. I'm going to answer it with fact number three. Ready?

Y: Yes.

L: Loch Ness was covered in ice until 18,000 years ago. This means that a prehistoric animal long believed extinct could not have been hiding in the lake for 66 million years. It would have had to be living somewhere else for most of that time. It couldn't have moved into the loch until the ice melted, sometime in the past 18,000 years. So where was it living before then? And why would it have migrated to a freezing cold lake? When the ice first melted, the water was even colder than it is now. And would a plesiosaur really have found Loch Ness hospitable? According to fossils found and studied by scientists, the plesiosaur was a tropical animal. The Scottish Highlands are NOT tropical.

Y: So maybe the monster isn't a plesiosaur. Maybe it's something else. Something that looks like a plesiosaur. Something *warm-blooded*.

L: It's a thought, but do you have any evidence?

Y: No. *[You pause.]* You've studied the loch for decades. Have you found any evidence?

L: Not a thing—no fossils, no skeletons, nothing.

Y: Have you ever seen something strange or mysterious while you were on the loch?

L: I wish! But no.

Y: *[You sigh.]*

L: I have seen other sights, though.

Y: Like what?

L: Have you ever heard of the thermocline effect?

Y: Sure. That's the layer between the warmer water on a lake's surface, and the colder water at the bottom.

L: That's right! On Loch Ness these layers of water are shifted by the summer wind, which blows consistently from the southwest. It actually pushes the warm layer of water toward the northeastern part of the lake. Then, when fall arrives and the wind dies down, the warm water begins moving back to the southwest. It does so in a see-saw motion, back and forth, back and forth. And these shifting layers of water can create huge underwater waves.

Y: So cool!

L: I know, right? Even cooler, these underwater waves form a surface current that can carry logs and other debris *against* the wind.

Y: You mean . . .

L: Yes! The wind can be huffing and puffing from the north, but a log caught in the lake's surface current can be bobbing along in the opposite direction, giving the effect of—

Y: *[You interrupt excitedly.]* A creature swimming against the current.

L: You can see how people might mistake that log for the tail or neck of a swimming creature. And that's not all. There are waterspouts on the loch, whirling columns of mist and air. They just pop up, with no warning, on days when the water is smooth as glass.

Y: Have you seen one yourself?

L: Plenty of times. Not long ago I was out on the loch when I heard this huge splash off to the right of my boat. I didn't catch the splash on my camera, but I did catch this huge spray coming off the water afterward. Want to see a waterspout?

Y: Yes, please!

[Once again, the sound of clicking keys is heard, followed by a ding indicating that you have received a text. You open it.]

Y: Wow, it kind of looks like the long neck of a thrashing beast.

L: I hadn't noticed that before.

Y: Could this be what Aldie MacKay saw? Did she see a waterspout? She claimed she saw a big splash. She called it a "commotion." And could the creature she later claimed to have seen swimming against the current have been some sort of debris caught in a thermocline-affected surface current?

L: What's more likely? Use Occam's Razor.

Y: Use what?

L: *[Gasps.]* Look at the time! I've got to run, but I've enjoyed our conversation.

Y: Thank you so much for your help. I really appreciate it.

L: You're very welcome. And good luck with your investigation.

[She hangs up.]

Your head is stuffed with information. You take a few minutes to write down all you've learned in your notebook. You've now got a long list of scientific facts. But you need to look one thing up: Occam's Razor.

11

FROM THE BLACK SWAN SCIENTIFIC INVESTIGATOR'S HANDBOOK

RAZOR-SHARP THINKING

When an event occurs, it is natural to wonder how it happened. The scientific principle of Occam's Razor indicates that the simplest answer is *often* the correct one. That does not mean it is *always* the correct answer. Good investigators look at *all* the evidence. But they should start with the answers that require the fewest assumptions. Below are some examples.

Mysterious Lights

You see a bright light flash through your curtains. What is it? Two possibilities come to mind:

- Lightning.

- UFO spaceship.

You're jumping to a lot of conclusions if you assume the bright light was caused by a UFO. These assumptions include the existence of extraterrestrial life, which so far is unproven. The lightning explanation requires only one assumption: a storm is coming. In an investigation, you would start by searching for evidence of a thunderstorm.

Conspiracy

You fail your spelling test. Two explanations spring to mind:

- You didn't study.

- Your teacher is a shape-shifter who sabotaged your grade because of your investigative work with BSSI.

Like most conspiracy theories, the shape-shifting saboteur explanation only works with LOTS of assumptions. You must assume your teacher is a shape-shifter and that he knows you work for BSSI. Additionally, you have to assume that he dislikes you (but not your classmates) enough to risk his job to bring your grade down. Occam's Razor indicates that your failure to study well enough is the better explanation in this case. To get to the bottom of the bad grade, you should start by looking at your study habits.

Crime Spree

You return to your remote mountain home after a long day's hunt for Bigfoot to find trash strewn all over. You consider two explanations:

- Your dog got into the trash.

- Bigfoot broke into your house and trashed it.

Your dog getting into the trash is the easiest explanation in this case. It requires far fewer assumptions than Bigfoot—whose existence remains unproven—breaking and entering. You begin your investigation by searching for evidence that the dog did it.

Mind Control

You've had a terrible headache all day. You search the internet and come up with two explanations:

- You are dehydrated.

- A microchip has secretly been implanted in your brain.

We've all been in situations where physical symptoms seem scary. It's easy to jump to terrifying conclusions. But deciding that a microchip has been inserted into your brain requires oodles more assumptions than deciding your headache is caused by dehydration. Start your investigation by drinking water. If your headache subsides, dehydration was the likeliest reason.

You consider all the sightings where Nessie was seen swimming in the lake—the MacKays' story, Hugh Gray's, even Dr. Wilson's. You use Occam's Razor. Which requires the fewest assumptions: A waterspout that naturally and commonly occurs on Loch Ness, or a prehistoric reptile that has been hiding from humankind for 66 million years?

Q

At last, you turn to George Spicer's sighting. His story is the most spectacular because he claimed to have seen Nessie up close and on land. It was also the first time anyone had made a connection between the monster and a prehistoric creature. In fact, Spicer said it looked very much like the dinosaur-type creature in *King Kong*.

There's only one thing to do. You make some popcorn, snuggle up on the sofa with Cosmos, and watch the black-and-white monster movie for yourself.

You get to a scene where a group of men are rowing a raft across a fog-shrouded lake. Something stirs in the water. A dark, snakelike neck breaks the surface, then slides back out of sight. Minutes later, the creature attacks, spilling the men into the lake. In a series of dramatic camera shots, the huge plesiosaur-like beast plucks the men out of the water and eats them. You can't help but notice that this monster, with its rounded back, arched neck, and small head, is almost identical to George Spicer's description. The men in the movie monster's mouth look like sheep. Didn't Spicer's beast have a sheep in its mouth?

You keep watching. A few of the men manage to escape. As they straggle onto shore, the creature chases them. And you realize it! Spicer almost exactly re-created this scene from the movie. Spicer said his monster crossed the road from left to right, just like the monster in *King Kong*. Just like in the movie, Spicer saw the monster's neck first, then its body. The movie monster even has elephant skin, just like Spicer's monster. Interestingly, in the movie, the creature's feet are not seen. Spicer claimed not to have seen his monster's feet either.

You turn off the movie. Did *King Kong* inspire George Spicer's sighting? If so, why? Was he a prankster? A storyteller? Did he misidentify something in the road? Or is the similarity between Spicer's monster and the movie monster just coincidence?

Mrs. Spicer backed up her husband. She claimed everything he said was true. They *had* seen something big crossing the road. Does that make the story more believable? Or could they both be lying?

George Spicer claimed to have gotten out of the car after the monster disappeared. He looked for physical evidence, but he didn't find anything. But wouldn't a ginormous animal have trampled the foliage that was on both sides of the road? Spicer says, however, that no plants were trampled. Is that possible?

There's no solid evidence to prove or disprove their story. All you have is some circumstantial evidence—George Spicer's monster looks a lot like the one from *King Kong*, a movie he saw. But is that enough? What should you believe? Can you take the Spicers' word for it? Should you?

You've come to the end of your case. You've used your investigative skills to ask good questions, gather evidence, and spot lies. Now you're ready to draw a conclusion.

You open your handbook one last time.

FROM THE BLACK SWAN SCIENTIFIC INVESTIGATOR'S HANDBOOK

YOUR CONCLUSION

Most people are good at jumping to conclusions. They will often base their decisions on emotions, past experiences, personal beliefs, and wishful thinking. But you know better. As a BSSI investigator, you never conclude a case without slowing down and evaluating all the evidence. You know that a solid conclusion should be:

1. Informed: It is based on good questions and a close examination of the answers.

2. Logical: It makes sense based on the gathered evidence.

3. Objective: It is free of opinions, assumptions, lies, and wishful thinking.

How can you reach a strong conclusion? Try the following:

1. Look for connections. Where does the evidence agree? Where does it disagree? **Example:** Three eyewitnesses claim to have seen a falling star in the night sky. A fourth witness, however, claims to have seen a spaceship. Based on the fact that most people saw a falling star, you can conclude that it was, indeed, a falling star.

2. Look for cause and effect. Has one event influenced another? Has one witness's testimony affected another's? **Example:** During a court trial, Mr. Smith testifies that on the night of a full moon, he saw a large cat running down his street. His next-door neighbor, Mr. Adams, testifies that a werewolf ran down the street. Mr. Smith approaches the judge. He explains he was mistaken. He *did* see a werewolf. You can conclude that Mr. Smith's new version was influenced by Mr. Adams's testimony, and that his new story is doubtful.

3. Compare your evidence against reliable sources. **Example:** Mrs. Arnold reports that a bat with a ten-foot wingspan swooped down as she left a convenience store and grabbed her soda. You contact a chiropterologist, a person who studies bats, who explains that bats that big do not exist anywhere on Earth. The bat with the biggest wingspan, she says, is the giant golden-crowned flying fox with a wingspan of five feet. She also adds that bats don't drink soda. You can conclude that Mrs. Arnold has a vivid imagination.

4. Check your conclusions for assumptions, opinions, and wishful thinking. **Example:** A fisherman claims to have found the preserved remains of a mermaid. The investigator on the case, a mermaid enthusiast, examines the remains. Under a magnifying glass, the investigator sees tiny stitch marks, indicating the remains had been sewn together. The investigator, however, is eager to prove that mermaids are real. Instead of questioning this evidence, her eagerness causes her to accept the remains as solid physical evidence. Because of this, the investigator will end up building her case on this flimsy evidence, which will result in a weak conclusion.

5. Verify that your conclusion makes sense with the evidence you've uncovered. **Example:** An investigator is on the trail of the yeti. Recently, a photographer hiking in the Himalayan Mountains snapped two pictures of the creature. The photographs were later analyzed by an anthropologist and proven genuine. Despite this, the investigator concludes that the creature was a bear. Conclusions that do not agree with the evidence will be weak.

6. Last but not least: The strongest conclusion is the one that makes the most sense and is based on the best evidence.

Hmmm . . . you've got a lot to think about. You ruffle Cosmos's ears. What does the evidence you uncovered tell you about the events of the 1930s?

It's time for you to draw your own conclusion.

Is the Loch Ness monster real?

PART THREE

13

SCIENCE HAS ITS SAY

You've drawn your conclusion. Perhaps the evidence led you to deduce that the 1930s monster was nothing more than a figment of people's imaginations. Or perhaps you judged that Nessie *does* swim beneath the loch's dark waters. You may even have decided that you couldn't reach a conclusion because you needed more evidence.

Lots of other Nessie investigators have longed for more evidence, too. Since the MacKays' sighting, there have been 1,157 (and counting) glimpses of Nessie, according to the "Official Loch Ness Monster Sightings Register." Curiously, most of these occurred *after* 1960. In fact, there was not one reported sighting of Nessie in the 1940s.

The first scientific attempt to settle the monster matter was made in 1934 by Sir Edward Mountain, who paid twenty men to stand at different locations around the loch. Each was supplied with binoculars and a camera. They watched for two weeks in July. The result of the experiment? This rather ordinary photograph showing some unusual waves. Many, including Sir Mountain, claimed they'd been made by the monster.

The reason? World War II.

When war erupted in 1939, British citizens turned their attention to fighting for their country. And when the conflict finally ended in 1945, they focused on rebuilding their lives. The Loch Ness monster was all but forgotten, until . . .

14

THE RETURN OF NESSIE

Dr. Constance Whyte's patients trusted her. They confided their secrets and shared personal details about their lives. They gossiped freely about their neighbors. And some told her tales of the monster in the loch.

Had they seen the creature themselves?

"We saw *two* monsters," claimed a witness. "They were on the [far] side of the loch at play."

"Its mouth was a foot wide," stated another, "and there were, on either side of its head, appendages comparable to a snail."

"It turned its head toward me," swore yet another. "I noticed something like a frill at the top of its neck. Its eyes were circular, large and glittering."

Dr. Whyte was intrigued. And although she never saw the monster herself, she came to believe in its existence. She began collecting accounts of Nessie sightings—dozens of them—and compiled them into a book titled *More Than a Legend: The Story of the Loch Ness Monster.*

The book, published in 1957, reignited the public's fascination with the mysterious creature and inspired a new generation of Nessie hunters. Wrote one reviewer, "If proof of the monster . . . can be accepted without it actually being caught and exhibited, this book presents the evidence in a way that is neat, objective and convincing."

But was it trustworthy evidence?

While the tales were entertaining, and at times exciting, Whyte refused to name her witnesses. Instead, she identified them by their initials only. She did this, she claimed, to save them from any public ridicule. She also left out important details like the dates, places, and times of the sightings. Both these unusual practices made it impossible for researchers to verify the accounts.

Additionally, there were many discrepancies in the witnesses' descriptions of the monster. Some described the beast as having a broad, smooth back, while others said it was humped. Some declared its neck snakelike; others said that it was short-necked. Some said it had horns. One witness even swore he saw smoke puffing from the monster's mouth. Whyte breezily explained away these inconsistencies. All this meant, she wrote, was that the witnesses were describing *different* monsters—"males, females, old and young."

Could there really be more than one monster in the loch?

Whyte also explained why Nessie had not been reported until 1933. It was because of the new road, she said. Completed that year, it gave drivers a clear view of the water. While most readers accepted this as fact, in truth, the road around the loch had been there for a hundred years *before* the MacKays' sighting.

The book ended with a plea from its author: "Someday the truth must surely be known. Why not start the investigation now?"

Why not, indeed, thought a young aeronautical engineer named Tim Dinsdale. He kept turning Whyte's story over in his mind. "I dreamt I walked the steep jutting shore and peered down at inky waters searching for the monster; waiting for it to burst from the depths . . . I awoke and knew that the imaginary search beginning in my dream had grown into fact."

So in April 1960, he packed up his movie camera and drove the nine hours from his home in Reading, England, to Loch Ness. His plan? To capture the monster on film.

THE DINSDALE FILM

Tim Dinsdale had been driving around Loch Ness for four days. The light was already fading when he saw what he described as a "churning of rough water, centering about what appeared to be two long black shadows, or shapes, rising and falling in the water!"

Dinsdale quickly trained his camera on the disturbance and filmed until the water calmed. Later he went to bed feeling, he admitted, as if he'd "grasped the monster by the tail."

His luck continued. On the morning of his sixth day at the loch, as he came up over a hill, he saw an object on the water's surface, about two-thirds of the way across the lake. "I dropped my binoculars and turned to my camera, and with deliberate and icy control began to film . . . as [the monster] swam across the loch it changed course, leaving a glassy zigzag wake; and then it slowly began to submerge."

Convinced of his success, Dinsdale returned home. When his motion pictures were developed, however, he discovered that his first film of Nessie was "no more than the wash and swirl of waves around a hidden shoal of rocks."

But what about the second film?

It showed an indistinct blob moving on the surface of the water a mile in the distance. And yet, Dinsdale truly believed he'd captured proof of the monster's existence—and felt that the world would soon agree. Unfortunately, even he had to admit that the film's quality was terrible. "It was a shabby little black and white image that traced its way across the screen," he said.

That didn't stop the film from becoming big news. Dinsdale's days were suddenly a whirlwind of TV and radio interviews. Still photographs from the film appeared in newspapers and magazines. He even secured a book deal. Both he and Nessie became monster celebrities.

Some people, however, remained skeptical. And so in 1966 Dinsdale arranged for the film to be analyzed by photographic experts working with Britain's Royal Air Force. They found that the moving blob was consistent in appearance and speed with a motorboat . . . and yet, the report continued, if the blob *was* a boat it surely would not have been missed by an observer. Therefore, maybe it was a living creature. While Dinsdale liked to think that the experts had authenticated his film, in truth, their conclusion wasn't helpful.

Since then, other experts have attempted to enhance the film. A faculty member at Virginia Tech's Computer Science Department scanned some of the film's frames at a higher resolution and examined it under various types of enhancing techniques. He concluded that the film does *not* show a boat.

In 2005, experts from the Royal Air Force reexamined the film. Using more modern technology this time around, they concluded that the object was a small boat being steered by a person.

Did Dinsdale really film the monster? The blob, sadly, cannot tell us—at least not for sure. Yet, his film is still considered by many monster hunters to be "the single best piece of photographic evidence of Nessie."

16

THE WATCHERS

Sparked by Dinsdale's film, a group of dedicated amateur investigators arrived at Loch Ness. Their goal was to find scientific evidence of the monster's existence. To this end, they formed the Loch Ness Investigation Bureau with the goal of systematically watching the water. By 1964, they were constantly surveilling large swaths of the loch.

A researcher with the Loch Ness Investigation Bureau sits atop a minibus, a camera trained on the water. The bureau had observation positions all around the loch in hopes of filming the monster.

They used giant movie cameras located in dozens of places around the shore that ran from dawn to dusk.

Researchers expected success. "Surely, seven days a week for five months would produce results," said member F. W. Holiday. "After all, if you watch a given area of sky long enough, you are bound to see a rainbow."

But while the group did get a rainbow on film, they did not catch Nessie.

The group persisted. They repeated the project for the next eight years . . . with the same results. No monster.

At last, in 1974, the group finally took down their cameras and the Loch Ness Investigation Bureau disbanded.

17

SUBS

In 1969, American inventor and adventurer Dan Taylor arrived at Loch Ness with a twenty-foot yellow submarine he called the *Viperfish*. He'd built the one-man craft in his spare time. Made of fiberglass, it couldn't go faster than eight miles an hour. Taylor, however, didn't care about speed. He planned to lurk near the loch's bottom, where he hoped to find the monster.

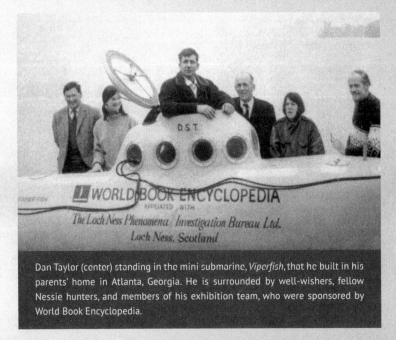

Dan Taylor (center) standing in the mini submarine, *Viperfish*, that he built in his parents' home in Atlanta, Georgia. He is surrounded by well-wishers, fellow Nessie hunters, and members of his exhibition team, who were sponsored by World Book Encyclopedia.

On one of Taylor's first runs, the *Viperfish* mysteriously twisted around on its own. A large cloud of silt rose from the loch floor. Taylor tried to see what was happening. But the loch's peaty water limited visibility to just a few feet. The monster—if it *was* the monster—disappeared into the murk. Said Taylor, "It wasn't until I was back on the surface and on dry land that it occurred to me that this might have been the monster saying hello."

Taylor made forty-five dives that summer. But he saw little more than the yellow glow of the *Viperfish*'s lights reflecting off the underwater gloom.

Other submariners tried to pick up where Taylor left off in 1973 and (as a tourist business) in 1994 and 1995. The murky, peat-silted water defeated them, too. Was there no way to see through the inky darkness?

18

SONAR

Between 1958 and 1970, four separate expeditions were launched, first by the British Broadcasting Company (the BBC), then by three highly respected British universities: Oxford, Cambridge, and the University of Birmingham. And each expedition came equipped with sonar.

Sonar, a technology developed by the military, uses sound to

A scientist uses a sonar device to try and locate the monster in 1989. The loch has been scanned multiple times. And still the mystery persists.

search underwater environments. Untroubled by peat-filled water, sonar allows you to see a mile or more down, making it easy to plumb the loch's deepest secrets. The trouble is, sometimes sonar will tell you things you *want* to hear rather than what is actually there. Sonar can bounce off underwater rocks, the wakes of boats, chains used to moor watercraft, and even the thermocline, that invisible boundary between layers of water at different temperatures. It also tends to bounce off the steep, rocky sides of the loch.

Perhaps this is what the University of Birmingham expedition picked up in 1968. Their team detected two large and moving underwater objects. Was it the monster? With high hopes, they returned the following year and found . . . nothing.

In 1972, Boston's Academy of Applied Science used sonar to map the floor of the loch's Urquhart Bay. There they found previously undiscovered ridges and canyons where monsters could easily hide. Too bad it wasn't true. The canyon and ridges were, in actuality, echoes from the loch's rocky sides.

Researchers from the Oxford-Cambridge expedition got less exciting results. After weeks of searching, a sonar technician admitted, "Nothing was detected . . . This seems to rule out the possibility that a large animal exists in Loch Ness."

And what of the BBC? They, too, came up empty-handed.

19

UNDERWATER CAMERAS

The loch's water was flat and calm on the morning of August 8, 1972. A sonar rig lay on the lake floor, thirty feet beneath the surface. So did a camera unit. Suddenly, at 1:40 a.m., the water's surface came alive with leaping salmon. Was something chasing them? Five minutes later, the sonar rig picked up something big and moving. The sonar rig triggered the camera unit. Instantly, the unit's strobe light began flashing as the camera snapped away.

But had it photographed anything?

At first light, Robert Rines, a Nessie hunter from Boston, pulled up the camera unit and shipped the film to New York to be developed. When the images came back, four of them showed something large and solid. But what was it? The quality was too hazy to tell. Rines wondered if the images could be enhanced.

In those days, when a mainframe computer filled an entire room, only a few places in the United States could enhance photographs. One of these places was the NASA Jet Propulsion Lab in Pasadena,

California. Rines sent his photographs there. Could the lab's technicians sharpen up the images?

The results flabbergasted Rines. While three of the images remained indistinct, the fourth showed . . .

A flipper!

Diamond-shaped, it was two to three feet across and six feet long. It was attached to a creature estimated by Rines to be thirty feet in length.

The image took the scientific world by storm. A meeting held at the British Museum of Natural History included an announcement that the flipper photograph was, indeed, genuine. Around the same time, an ichthyologist at the Smithsonian in Washington, DC, agreed that the images showed flipper-like appendages. And the head of the New England Aquarium in Boston declared the flippers unlike anything else known to humankind. They could only, he declared, belong to an unknown species. Not to be outdone, a well-known paleontologist demonstrated how the flipper in the photo resembled that of a plesiosaur.

When taken together, the flipper photo and the Dinsdale film provided compelling evidence of Nessie's existence. Some researchers were so convinced that they pressured the scientific community to give the monster a binomial name (a two-part Latin name for a species of *living* organism). They proposed *Nessiteras rhombopteryx,* meaning "Ness monster with diamond-shaped wings." By giving it a proper scientific name, they hoped to have Nessie declared an endangered species, and thus granted protection. "Better . . . to be safe than sorry," they argued, ". . . a name for a species whose existence is still a matter of controversy among scientists is preferable to none if its protection is to be assured."

For the next fifteen years, Rines and his discoveries continued to confound the scientific world. In June 1975 he took two more extraordinary photographs. The first showed the monster's head, neck, and front flippers. The second showed a creature's neck and head, complete with horns. Dr. Roy Mackal, a biochemist at the University of Chicago, believed the photo was positive proof that the monster existed. These new images, plus the flipper photo, were published in *Nature* magazine, one of the foremost scientific journals in the world. Nessie believers considered the article a triumph. Finally, they thought, the often narrow-minded scientific community was taking them seriously.

In 1984, a group of researchers took another look at the flipper photo. Curious about the enhancement techniques used on it, they examined the original image, the one Rines sent to the Jet Propulsion Lab. What it showed was a greenish, blurry mess. Researchers did *not* see a flipper.

Next, they corresponded with Alan Gillespie, the technician who had computer-enhanced the original image. Gillespie stated that the image he saw in *Nature* magazine was *not* the processed image he'd worked on. His enhanced image had shown a vague diagonal line that was slightly brighter than the background. There was absolutely no hint of anything diamond-shaped.

Researchers returned to the enhanced image. A large blowup of this version revealed something surprising: paintbrush marks. In those days before Photoshop, someone had taken a fine paintbrush and created an edge of darkness and a perfect flipper out of the photographic mess.

When confronted with these facts, Rines acted shocked. He claimed he knew nothing about it. He'd been duped just like everyone else.

The flipper photo was a fake, meant to deceive. But what about the original image? It showed something large and solid. Could it have been Nessie?

20

"OPERATION DEEPSCAN"

Adrian Shine started chasing the monster at the age of twenty-three. By 1987, he'd been at it for over a third of his life. In that time, he'd earned a reputation as a serious scientist. He'd also gone from enthusiastic believer to a man whose faith in monsters was slipping away. And yet, he still hoped against the odds that Nessie would be found.

That's why he'd decided to launch "Operation Deepscan." Large and ambitious, the project, Shine hoped, would once and for all answer the monster question. A comb that no large animal could evade would be dragged through the water from one end of the loch to the other. The comb would be nine hundred yards across and have broad, flat teeth made of sonar beams directed at the loch's floor from a line of boats advancing in unison.

On October 9, after five days of training, twenty boats equipped with high-resolution tracking sonar lined up fifty yards apart. Slowly, they moved across the water. Any unusual sonar findings were marked with a buoy. Then a message was sent to the response boat, *New Atlantis*, waiting behind the line. It was *New Atlantis*'s job to investigate the findings.

The flotilla cruised in formation down the middle of the loch to Fort Augustus at its southwest end. The next morning, it cruised back. In that time, three unusual findings were recorded. Whatever had caused the sonar blips had disappeared by the time *New Atlantis* reached the spots. Shine believed two of the findings were false—sonar echoes off rocks or boat wakes. But the third remained a mystery. It was "smaller than a whale but larger than a shark," over five hundred feet down and apparently diving.

Had "Operation Deepscan" picked up Nessie?

21

DREDGING AND CORE SAMPLING

It stands to reason that if monsters live, they must also die. If a population of creatures has been living in the loch since the glacier melted 18,000 years ago (or even since the MacKays' sighting in 1933), they would surely have left bones on the loch's floor. But the 1969 submarine didn't see any. Neither did two submarines that trolled the waters in the mid-1990s. Of course, the water's inkiness makes it difficult to see anything below the surface.

So, researchers used scoops, dredges, and core samplers in hopes of finding skeletal remains. From the 1970s to the 1990s, they plumbed the silt-covered, flat floor of Loch Ness. No monster bones were found. But a great deal was learned about the life of the loch—from fish to plankton. Researchers even discovered an invasive species of American flatworm thought to have been brought in on monster-hunting equipment. What else was discovered? A scientific treasure of a different kind. Researchers learned that the deep, even, and undisturbed sediment on the loch's floor is a delicate and stratified geologic record of the region. It provides a natural history that goes all the way back to the time of the glaciers. To preserve this resource, all dredging for monster bones has stopped.

Other researchers argue that a lack of bones doesn't mean Nessie isn't real.

What if the creature is a boneless invertebrate like a snail or an octopus? Then the monster's remains would be quickly scavenged away by fish and birds.

Or what about the acidity level of the loch's water? Says researcher Dick Raynor, "Exposed bones are not likely to survive many years . . . as the loch will cause them to dissolve and crumble in the slightly acidic environment." It has been estimated that it would take just fifty years for the largest bone in a plesiosaur body to dissolve in Loch Ness.

Or what if Nessie only visits the loch? What if she lives somewhere else?

22

HIDDEN TUNNELS AND CAVES

It has long been speculated that Loch Ness is connected to the North Sea by underwater caves and tunnels. This might explain the lack of bones. It would also explain the absence of sonar evidence. "In the case of a single occasional migrant, [sonar] detection would be virtually impossible," admits one researcher. But is there any evidence that tunnels exist? Monster hunters have found none.

However, in 2023, the *Inverness Courier* (the same newspaper that broke the MacKay sighting) reported that Paige Daley, who runs the TikTok Official Loch Ness Channel, made a dramatic claim: She had found an underground cave system during a recent expedition to Loch Ness. Where is it? Daley said she was keeping the location secret "for fear of disturbing whatever creature or creatures might be there." She did add that the caves had multiple entrances and were linked to the loch by a short stretch of the River Ness.

Skeptical researchers note that the River Ness is well-traveled and broken by shipping locks. Wouldn't a large monster be spied as it made its way to and from the loch? Also, at some times of the year, the river is so shallow that fishermen can wade across it. Additionally, the river runs smack dab through the city of Inverness. Perhaps, they suggest, there is an additional and more secret route?

23

SCAN IT AGAIN

In the summer of 2003, a research team funded by the British Broadcasting Company (BBC) arrived at Loch Ness. And this time, using modern-day technology—sonar beams and satellite navigation technology—they tackled the inky water. Not an inch of the loch was left unexamined.

"We went from shoreline to shoreline, top to bottom on this one, we have covered everything in the loch," said one of the specialists carrying out the project. They did find a buoy moored several feet below the surface. But, they say, "no signs of any large living animal."

Added his colleague, "We got some good clear data of the loch, steep-sided, flat-bottomed—nothing unusual, I'm afraid."

The team concluded that the Loch Ness monster is a myth and that people see what they want to see.

To prove this, researchers rigged up a fence post beneath the surface of the loch. When a busload of tourists arrived, they raised the post. Many of the tourists gasped and pointed. Some took pictures.

Later, the researchers interviewed the tourists. They asked them to draw what they had just seen. Some observed nothing more than a square object. But many sketched a monster-shaped head. They appeared disappointed to learn they'd seen nothing more than a fence post.

Both skeptics and Nessie believers agree that many reported sightings are due to misidentification. Says one researcher, "At Loch Ness, the opportunities to be deceived are legion." Common objects, known animals, and natural phenomena can create an illusion of Nessie, especially for those hoping to see it. In fact, Dr. Roy Mackal, the biochemist at the University of Chicago, concluded that a whopping 90 percent of all sightings could be identified as mistakes, misinterpretation, or fraud. And there are many documented cases where witnesses mistook objects or animals for Nessie.

Researcher John Kirk remembered his first trip to Loch Ness. He stood gazing hopefully out at the water when a long, slender neck popped out of the water.

"The hair on the back of my neck stood up," Kirk recalled.

Luckily, Kirk's binoculars hung around his neck. He put them up to his eyes and saw . . .

"A crested grebe, a common waterfowl frequently responsible for causing false alarms in the lake."

More than birds are seen in the loch. So, too, are otters, dolphins, and seals. Joe Nickell, a legendary monster hunter, believes otters account for many Nessie sightings. Not only do otters live around the loch, but their long, sinuous necks and snakelike heads resemble those of plesiosaurs. Their rolling dives can create the illusion of undulating waves. And a group of otters swimming together can look like one large creature.

Seals and dolphins also venture into the loch on occasion. Despite being marine animals, they have been known to follow the salmon up the River Ness. Seals have even been known to live in the loch for months at a time.

Could Nessie be a visiting seal?

Or is the monster a . . .

GIGANTIC EEL

Dr. Neil Gemmell, a geneticist from the University of Otago in New Zealand, had an idea. Why not test the genetic material of DNA present in the water of Loch Ness? He wouldn't have to capture any creatures to do this. All he needed were water samples that had gotten close to the organisms living in the loch. He would collect any small particles shed by the creatures, and then concentrate and sequence them. Finally, he would compare the DNA found in the loch to an international data bank to figure out what species lived in the mysterious water.

In June of 2018, Gemmell and his team crisscrossed the loch for two weeks, collecting hundreds of water samples from the surface and depths of the loch. After returning to their lab, they began sequencing and comparing. "Right from the get-go, I said I don't believe in the monster," said Gemmell. "But wouldn't it be amazing if I was wrong?"

Eventually, the researchers found evidence of three thousand species in the water, including fish, deer, pigs, birds, humans, bacteria, and eels. Lots and lots of eels. Almost every water sample had European eel in it.

Could Nessie sightings have actually been sightings of eels that had grown to an extreme size? Gemmell couldn't rule out the theory. "We don't know if the eel DNA we are detecting is from gigantic eels, or just many small eels."

Was it possible that, for whatever reason, some eels in the loch grew supersized?

Certainly, there have been stories about eels in Loch Ness. According to one professional diver, the snakelike creatures

Dr. Neil Gemmell takes water samples from Loch Ness on June 11, 2018, in hopes of sequencing the DNA of the creatures who live in the water.

swarmed him when he reached the loch floor. He refused to dive there ever again. Another workman told how a nearby hydro plant became clogged with eels, forcing it to shut down. Workers had to chop the eels out of the machinery. Some, he claimed, were as thick as a man's leg.

The European eel. Could Nessie be an oversized member of this species?

Like claims of the monster, however, these sightings came without physical evidence. There were no photos of the big eels, no specimens caught.

In fact, the biggest European eel ever caught was only three-and-a-half feet long and weighed fifteen pounds. "It doesn't sound like a monster, does it?" said Gemmell. Still, he couldn't rule out the big eel theory.

He was, however, able to rule out the theory that Nessie is a plesiosaur. His team found no evidence of *any* reptile DNA—no lizards, snakes, or turtles. They also didn't find any amphibians, like frogs and toads. "I think we can be fairly sure there is not a giant scaly reptile swimming around in Loch Ness," he concluded.

But could he have missed something? Why hadn't his study found the presence of otters or seals in Loch Ness? These animals are known to be in the water.

"We may have missed things," admitted Gemmell.

Things like Nessie?

Data scientist Floe Foxon can't answer that last question. But he has taken on Gemmell's big eel theory by examining it statistically. He studied the number of eels (around twenty thousand) caught in Loch Ness and in other lakes in Europe—their length, weight, and frequency of catches. This enabled him to calculate the odds of finding eels of various sizes.

So what does he say the odds are of finding a giant eel in Loch Ness?

Essentially zero. Even the chance of finding a three-foot eel there is low, about one in fifty thousand. And once you get much bigger than that, the probability plummets. Bottom line: Foxon believes the eel theory should "join the discard pile."

Too bad, though. "I really wish there was a giant eel in Loch Ness," Foxon said. But he insists wishes don't matter when one is searching for the truth. "[One] should approach these things with an open mind and let the data influence the decision-making."

25

THE BIGGEST SEARCH FOR NESSIE IN FIFTY YEARS

There were drones with infrared cameras. There was surveying equipment and sonar. There were spotters on land and boats with hydrophones listening for Nessie-like calls underwater. It was August 2023, and one hundred volunteers from all over the world had gathered at Loch Ness to hunt for signs of the monster. Another three hundred signed up to monitor a live stream of the loch and the search.

They searched systematically. Volunteers, placed in seventeen locations around the lake, monitored the water for Nessie. Meanwhile, others took out boats equipped with sonar and hydrophones. In one instance, searchers heard strange noises beneath the waves. In another, a volunteer photographed a large shadow circling in the water. There were also a few sightings of hump-shaped objects moving in and out of the loch, and an eel-like creature on its surface.

But despite the use of the most modern technologies, none of these sightings could be verified as Nessie.

"We are all looking for breaks in the surface and asking volunteers to record all manner of natural behavior on the loch," said search leader Alan McKenna, a member of Loch Ness Exploration, an amateur research team. "Not every ripple or wave is a beastie. Some of those can be explained, but there are a handful that cannot."

McKenna got excited when he heard "four distinctive 'gloops.'" Was that the sound of the monsters? His team ran to make sure the recorder was on. Sadly, it wasn't plugged in.

Without the recording, the search came away empty-handed.

But as leading Nessie authority Adrian Shine says, "Absence of evidence is not evidence of absence."

The searching and sightings continue.

26

PEOPLE STILL SEE . . . SOMETHING

It's been almost one hundred years since the MacKays first reported seeing something in the loch. Since then scientists and monster hunters alike have scanned, dredged, filmed, and tested the waters. But no definitive evidence has been found. And yet, people continue to see Nessie:

"I am a man of science so I never believed that the Loch Ness monster was a prehistoric animal. But when I was taking a picture [from the loch's shore] I saw this long, long shadow . . . I thought maybe it was a cloud, but there were none, or a boat, but none was near. There were small waves, like something was moving. It was 15–20 meters long and about 150 meters away. It was quite strange and then it disappeared."
—Etienne Camel sighting, June 15, 2023

"It looked exactly like a periscope but then two curved areas followed. It was moving and about half way out in the loch. . . . I can only describe

it as Nessie as I can't think of any logical thing it could have been. It was large enough to catch my eye and leave a slight wake behind it . . . The water was flat calm and there was no nearby boat activity. It lasted about 30–40 seconds."

—Fiona Wade sighting, August 31, 2023

"I was near the castle with my family about 1 p.m. when I noticed a little movement in the water. Then the water started to move a bit more and a long shape came out of the water. He wasn't green which I thought he would be, he was more a dark gray color. Then it went quickly away again but as it was going back under I could see a longer body. I don't know how long it was but it looked really long."

—Jarod Strong sighting, October 21, 2023

"At first thought was driftwood, but slowly but surely made it's [sic] *way north towards the castle. Looked like a head above the waves. Was difficult to determine with the naked eye."*

—Parry Malm sighting, April 4, 2024

And so . . .

The search goes on.

The sightings continue.

The theories multiply

And Nessie swims on, swift and elusive, in the imagination of millions.

Is it real?

Your adventure doesn't end here. The world is full of mysteries. And your next assignment is already on its way.

This picture, while obviously not real, sums up the hopes of millions: Nessie and baby swimming on ... at least in our imaginations.

BIBLIOGRAPHY

PRIMARY SOURCES
BOOKS

Gould, Rupert T., *The Loch Ness Monster and Others*, 1934; repr., Secaucus, NJ: Citadel Press, 1976.

Whyte, Constance, *More Than a Legend: The Story of the Loch Ness Monster*, London: H. Hamilton, 1957.

OTHER DOCUMENTS AND VIDEOS

Camel, Etienne, "The Official Loch Ness Sightings Register," https://www.lochnesssightings.com.

Dunn, Dennis, "*King Kong* Caps the Lot," *Daily Express* (London), April 19, 1933, 6.

Gemmell, Neil, "Loch Ness Monster Hunt Using Environmental DNA to (Hopefully) Sort Myth from Science," Australian Broadcasting Corporation, June 27, 2018, https://www.abc.net.au/news/2018-06-28/loch-ness-monster-hunt-nessie-scotland-environmental-dna/9918638.

"Leslie Holmes (1934)," British Pathé, 1934, YouTube video, https://www
.youtube.com/watch?v=_G5NArDuK2M.

"The Loch Ness Monster," *Nature*, December 16, 1934, https://www.nature
.com/articles/134765a0.

"London Surgeon's Photo of the Monster," *Daily Mail* (London), April 21,
1934, 1.

Malm, Parry, "The Official Loch Ness Sightings Register," https://www
.lochnesssightings.com.

"Monster Mystery Deepens," *Daily Mail* (London), January 4, 1934, 1.

"Mr. Wetherell and a Broadcast," *Daily Express* (London), December 23,
1933, 10.

"Naming the Loch Ness Monster," *Nature*, December 21, 1975, https://www
.nature.com/articles/258466a0.pdf.

"Report of Strange Spectacle on Loch Ness in 1933 Leaves Unanswered
Question—What Was It?" *Inverness Courier*, September 11, 2017, https://
www.inverness-courier.co.uk/news/report-of-strange-spectacle-on-loch
-ness-in-1933-leaves-unanswered-question-what-was-it-139582.

Strong, Jarod, "The Official Loch Ness Sightings Register," https://www
.lochnesssightings.com.

Wade, Fiona, "The Official Loch Ness Sightings Register," https://www
.lochnesssightings.com.

SECONDARY SOURCES
BOOKS

Bauer, Henry, *Enigma of Loch Ness: Making Sense of a Mystery*. Urbana: University of Illinois Press, 1986.

Coleman, Loren, and Patrick Huyghe, *The Field Guide to Lake Monsters, Sea Serpents, and Other Denizens of the Deep*, New York: Penguin/Tarcher, 2003.

Dinsdale, Tim, *Loch Ness Monster*, London: Routledge and Kegan Paul, 1961.

Holiday, F. W., *The Great Orm of Loch Ness: A Practical Inquiry into the Nature and Habits of Water-Monsters*, New York: Norton, 1969.

Loxton, Daniel, and Donald R. Prothero, *Abominable Science! Origins of the Yeti, Nessie, and Other Famous Cryptids*, New York: Columbia University Press, 2013.

Martin, David, and Alistair Boyd, *Nessie: The Surgeon's Photograph Exposed*, London: Thorne, 1999.

Williams, Gareth, *A Monstrous Commotion: The Mysteries of Loch Ness*, London: Orion Books, 2015.

NEWSPAPER AND MAGAZINE ARTICLES

"BBC 'Proves' Nessie Does Not Exist," BBC News, July 27, 2003, http://news .bbc.co.uk/2/hi/science/nature/3096839.stm.

Bernstein, Adam, "Dan Taylor, Loch Ness Hunter, Dies at 65," *Washington*

Post, August 4, 2005, http://washingtonpost.com/archive/local/2005/08 /04/dan-taylor-loch-ness-hunter-dies-at-65/32fb38d4-8f30-430a-a2ac -163949cbe7ca.

Dixon, Emily, "Loch Ness Monster Might Be Giant Eel, Scientists Say," CNN Travel, September 6, 2019, https://www.cnn.com/travel/article/loch-ness -monster-explanation-scli-intl/index.html.

"Hundreds Join Huge Search for the Loch Ness Monster," BBC, August 26, 2023, https://www.bbc.com/news/uk-scotland-highlands-islands-66614935.

Jolly, Peter, "Loch Ness Monster's Lair Discovered as New Cave System Revealed," *Daily Record*, August 23, 2023, https://www.dailyrecord.co.uk /news/scottish-news/loch-ness-monsters-lair-discovered-30770823.

Metcalfe, Tom, "Loch Ness Contains No 'Monster' DNA, Say Scientists," *Live Science*, September 9, 2019, https://www.livescience.com/loch-ness -monster-dna-study.html.

Newcomb, Tim, "A Mass Search Party Just Searched for the Loch Ness Monster. They Heard 4 'Gloops,'" *Popular Mechanics*, August 29, 2023, https://www .popularmechanics.com/science/a44927101/loch-ness-monster-search -gloops.

Rosen, Meghan, "Seen Bigfoot or the Loch Ness Monster? Data Suggest the Odds Are Low," *Science News*, September 26, 2023, https://www.science -news.org/article/bigfoot-loch-ness-monster-data-pseudoscience.

Shine, Adrian J., and David S. Martin, "Loch Ness Habitats Observed by Sonar and Underwater Television," Reprinted from *The Scottish Naturalist*, 1988. Previously published by the International Society of Cryptozoology, Society for the History of Natural History, Symposium on the Loch Ness Monster, Royal Museum of Scotland, Edinburgh, July 25, 1987.

Stagnaro, Angelo, "St. Columba and the Loch Ness Monster," *National Catholic Register*, https://www.ncregister.com/blog/st-columba-and-the-loch-ness -monster.

Starr, Michelle, "What If the Loch Ness Monster Was Actually a Giant Eel," *Science Alert*, July 25, 2023, https://www.sciencealert.com/what-if-the-loch -ness-monster-was-actually-a-giant-eel.

Watson, Roland, "Empirical Analysis of the Hugh Gray 'Nessie' Photograph," *Journal of Scientific Exploration*, August 20, 2022, https//doi.org/10.31275 /2022549.

Weaver, Matthew, "Loch Ness Monster Could Be a Giant Eel, Scientists Say," *The Guardian*, September 5, 2019, https://www.theguardian.com/science /2019/sep/05/loch-ness-monster-could-be-a-giant-eel-say -scientists.

OTHER DOCUMENTS AND VIDEOS

"Nessie on Land: The Spicers Story," *Loch Ness Mystery* (blog), August 21, 2017. https://lochnessmystery.blogspot.com/2017/08/nessie-on-land-spicers story.html.

SOURCE NOTES

PART ONE: THE INVESTIGATION BEGINS
THE FIRST SIGHTING, ALDIE AND JOHN MACKAY: APRIL 1933

"Strange Spectacle": "Report of Strange Spectacle on Loch Ness in 1933 Leaves Unanswered Question—What Was It?" *Inverness Courier*, September 11, 2017, https://www.inverness-courier.co.uk/news/report-of-strange-spectacle-on-loch -ness-in-1933-leaves-unanswered-question-what-was-it-139582.

"water beast": Angelo Stagnaro, "St. Columba and the Loch Ness Monster," *National Catholic Register*, https://www.ncregister.com/blog/st-columba -and-the-loch-ness-monster.

THE SECOND SIGHTING, GEORGE SPICER: JULY 22, 1933

"George, what on earth": "Nessie On Land: The Spicers Story," *Loch Ness Mystery* (blog), August 21, 2017. https://lochnessmystery.blogspot.com /2017/08/nessie-on-land-spicers-story.html.

"diplodocus-like dinosaur": ibid.

"white and breathing": Dennis Dunn, "*King Kong* Caps the Lot," *Daily Express* (London), April 19, 1933, 6.

"much resembled": "Nessie On Land: The Spicers Story," *Loch Ness Mystery* (blog), August 21, 2017, https://lochnessmystery.blogspot.com/2017/08 /nessie-on-land-spicers-story.html.

THE THIRD SIGHTING, HUGH GRAY: NOVEMBER 12, 1933

"I did not see": Roland Watson, "Empirical Analysis of the Hugh Gray 'Nessie' Photograph," *Journal of Scientific Exploration*, August 20, 2022, https://doi.org/10.31275/2022549.

MORE CLUES?: DECEMBER 1933

"It is suggested": "Mr. Wetherell and a Broadcast," *Daily Express* (London), December 23, 1933, 10.

THE MONSTER BUBBLE BURSTS: JANUARY 4, 1934

"definitely created": "Monster Mystery Deepens," *Daily Mail* (London), January 4, 1934, 1.

"mounted specimen": ibid.

THE MONSTER RETURNS: APRIL 21, 1934

"London Surgeon's Photo": "London Surgeon's Photo of the Monster," *Daily Mail* (London), April 21, 1934, 1.

"It was the head": ibid.

PART TWO: YOU INVESTIGATE

"It's not genuine": David Martin and Alistair Boyd, *Nessie: The Surgeon's Photograph Exposed,* London: Thorne, 1999, 20.

"All right": ibid., 17.

"violent commotion": Rupert T. Gould, *The Loch Ness Monster and Others,* 1934; repr., Secaucus, NJ: Citadel Press, 1976, 39.

"two ducks fighting": ibid.

"Apparently it was caused": ibid., 40.

"the cause of the wake": ibid.

"The two humps": ibid.

"no traces of fins": ibid.

"swimming in a half-circle": ibid.

"self-advertising": ibid.

PART THREE: SCIENCE HAS ITS SAY
THE RETURN OF NESSIE

"We saw *two*": Constance Whyte, *More Than a Legend: The Story of the Loch Ness Monster,* London: H. Hamilton, 1957, 173.

"Its mouth was": ibid., 177.

"It turned its head": ibid., 203.

"If proof": ibid., front flap.

"males, females": ibid., 179.

"Someday the truth": ibid., 218

"I dreamt": Tim Dinsdale, *Loch Ness Monster*, London: Routledge and Kegan Paul, 1961, 5–6.

THE DINSDALE FILM

"churning of rough water": ibid., 95–96.

"grasped the monster": ibid., 110.

"I dropped my binoculars": ibid., 110.

"no more than": ibid.

"It was a shabby": ibid.

"the single best": Loren Coleman and Patrick Huyghe, *The Field Guide to Lake Monsters, Sea Serpents, and Other Denizens of the Deep*. New York: Penguin/Tarcher, 2003, 21.

THE WATCHERS

"Surely, seven days a week": F. W. Holiday, *The Great Orm of Loch Ness: A Practical Inquiry into the Nature and Habits of Water-Monsters*, New York: Norton, 1969, 64–65.

SUBS

"It wasn't until": Adam Bernstein, "Dan Taylor, Loch Ness Hunter, Dies at 65," *Washington Post*, August 4, 2005, http://washingtonpost.com/archive/local/2005/08/04/dan-taylor-loch-ness-hunter-dies-at-65/32fb38d4-8f30-430a-a2ac-163949cbe7ca.

SONAR

"Nothing was detected": Holiday, 201.

UNDERWATER CAMERAS

"Ness monster with": "Naming the Loch Ness Monster," *Nature*, December 21,

1975, https://www.nature.com/articles/258466a0.pdf.

"Better to be safe": ibid.

"OPERATION DEEPSCAN"

"smaller than a whale": Gareth Williams, *A Monstrous Commotion: The Mysteries of Loch Ness*, London: Orion Books, 2015, 201.

DREDGING AND CORE SAMPLING

"Exposed bones are not likely to survive . . .": https://lochnessmystery.blogspot .com/2014/05/the-carcass-problem-part-2.html.

HIDDEN TUNNELS AND CAVES

"In the case of a single occasional migrant . . .": Adrian J. Shine and David S. Martin, "Loch Ness Habitats Observed by Sonar and Underwater Television," International Society of Cryptozoology, Society for the History of Natural History, Symposium on the Loch Ness Monster, Royal Museum of Scotland, Edinburgh, July 25, 1987. Quoted in *The Scottish Naturalist*, 1988, 181.

"for fear of disturbing whatever creature . . .": Peter Jolly, "Loch Ness Monster's Lair Discovered as New Cave System Revealed," *Daily Record*, August 23, 2023, https://www.dailyrecord.co.uk/news/scottish-news/loch-ness-monsters-lair -discovered-30770823.

SCAN IT AGAIN

"We went from shoreline": "BBC 'Proves' Nessie Does Not Exist," *BBC News*, July 27, 2003, http://news.bbc.co.uk/2/hi/science/nature/3096839.stm.

"We got some": ibid.

"At Loch Ness": Henry Bauer, *Enigma of Loch Ness: Making Sense of a Mystery*, Urbana: University of Illinois Press, 1986, 56.

"The hair on the back": Daniel Loxton and Donald R. Prothero, *Abominable Science! Origins of the Yeti, Nessie, and Other Famous Cryptids,* New York: Columbia University Press, 2013, ch. 4, loc. 3249.

"A crested grebe": ibid.

GIGANTIC EEL

"Right from the get-go": Tom Metcalfe, "Loch Ness Contains No 'Monster' DNA, Say Scientists," *Live Science*, September 9, 2019, https://www .livescience.com/loch-ness-monster-dna-study.html.

"We don't know": Matthew Weaver, "Loch Ness Monster Could Be a Giant Eel, Scientists Say," *The Guardian*, September 5, 2019, https://www.theguardian .com/science/2019/sep/05/loch-ness-monster-could-be-a-giant-eel-say-scientists.

"It doesn't sound": ibid.

"I think we can": Emily Dixon, "Loch Ness Monster Might Be Giant Eel, Scientists Say," CNN Travel, September 6, 2019, https://www.cnn.com/travel/article /loch-ness-monster-explanation-scli-intl/index.html.

"We may have": ibid.

"join the discard pile": Michelle Starr, "What If the Loch Ness Monster Was Actually a Giant Eel," *Science Alert*, July 25, 2023, https://www .sciencealert.com/what-if-the-loch-ness-monster-was-actually-a-giant-eel.

"I really wish": Meghan Rosen, "Seen Bigfoot or the Loch Ness Monster? Data Suggest the Odds Are Low," *Science News*, September 26, 2023, https://www .sciencenews.org/article/bigfoot-loch-ness-monster-data-pseudoscience.

"[One] should approach": Starr, https://www.sciencealert.com/what-if-the -loch-ness-monster-was-actually-a-giant-eel.

THE BIGGEST SEARCH FOR NESSIE IN FIFTY YEARS

"We are all looking": "Hundreds Join Huge Search for the Loch Ness Monster," BBC, August 26, 2023, https://www.bbc.com/news/uk-scotland-highlands -islands-66614935.

"four distinctive 'gloops.'": Tim Newcomb, "A Mass Search Party Just Searched for the Loch Ness Monster. They Heard 4 'Gloops,'" *Popular Mechanics*, August 29, 2023, https://www.popularmechanics.com/science/a44927101 /loch-ness-monster-search gloops/.

"Absence of evidence": Neil Gemmell, "Loch Ness Monster Hunt Using Environmental DNA to (Hopefully) Sort Myth from Science," Australian Broadcasting Corporation, June 27, 2018, https://www.abc.net.au/news /2018-06-28/loch-ness-monster-hunt-nessie-scotland-environmental-dna /9918638.

PEOPLE STILL SEE . . . SOMETHING

"I am a man": Etienne Camel, "The Official Loch Ness Sightings Register," https://www.lochnesssightings.com.

"It looked exactly like": Fiona Wade, ibid.

"I was near": Jarod Strong, ibid.

"At first thought": Parry Malm, ibid.

PHOTOGRAPH AND ILLUSTRATION CREDITS

Photos ©: vii, 26, 44, 46, 49 bottom left: Pictorial Press Ltd/Alamy Stock Photo; 3: Travel Scotland - Paul White/Alamy Stock Photo; 7: Keith Corrigan/Alamy Stock Photo; 9, 59 center: Library of Congress; 11: Eric Rohmann; 12: Masheter Movie Archive/Alamy Stock Photo; 13: Archive PL/Alamy Stock Photo; 14: Corey Ford/Alamy Stock Photo; 16, 41, 44: Trinity Mirror/Mirrorpix/Alamy Stock Photo; 19: Daily Mail/Shutterstock; 22: Chronicle/Alamy Stock Photo; 28, 49 top and bottom right: Chronicle /Alamy Stock Photo; 39: The Loch Ness Centre; 45 top: NASA/JPL /University of Arizona; 45 bottom: Algis Motuza/Alamy Stock Photo; 51: Eric Rohmann; 58 bottom: John MacPherson/Alamy Stock Photo; 70: Eric Rohmann; 74: Dr. Joseph Golden/NOAA; 80: Moviestore Collection Ltd /Alamy Stock Photo; 88: Chronicle/Alamy Stock Photo; 95: Sueddeutsche Zeitung Photo/Alamy Stock Photo; 97: PA Images/Alamy Stock Photo; 99: Tom Stoddart Archive/Hulton Archive/Getty Images; 115: Andy Buchanan/AFP via Getty Images; 124–125: Chroma Collection/Alamy Stock Photo. All other photos © Shutterstock.com.

IS IT REAL?

THE LOCH NESS MONSTER

ABOUT THE AUTHOR

Candace Fleming is the versatile and acclaimed author of more than twenty books for children and young adults, including *The Enigma Girls: How Ten Teenagers Broke Ciphers, Kept Secrets, and Helped Win World War II*, which garnered six starred reviews; *Crash from Outer Space: Unraveling the Mystery of Flying Saucers, Alien Beings, and Roswell*; *The Curse of the Mummy: Uncovering Tutankhamun's Tomb*; *The Rise and Fall of Charles Lindbergh*, winner of the YALSA Excellence in Nonfiction for Young Adults Award; and the *Los Angeles Times* Book Prize winner and Sibert Honor Book *The Family Romanov: Murder, Rebellion, and the Fall of the Russian Empire*; among many others. She lives outside Chicago and can be found online at candacefleming.com.

LOOK FOR THESE EXCITING TRUE STORIES
BY CANDACE FLEMING!